JEANNE GRAFF

VZSZHHZZ

semiotext(e)

1.

Patrick comes to Le Bar for the first time in 1979, 27 rue de Condé. He takes it over in 1991. Since then, he has said that he was taken hostage by the place. Guattari lives a bit further down the street number 9. I come there for the first time in 2012. I ask Patrick if I can charge my phone behind the counter, then I draw his portrait— with open shirt as always and his silver chain—as well as those of three other customers. We really get along with each other right away. The portrait is still hanging on the frame of the mirror, which is at the right side at the entrance of the bar. Because I forget my phone when I leave, I have to come back the day after. Since then, I come back here often when I'm in Paris, if I want it to be quiet, to know no one. One evening, the customers at the table next to us—hardly 18 years old—order Patrick's famous cocktail "the crazy hand," a mix of *liqueurs flambé* shaken with a hand that covers the top of the cognac glass. They first breathe the alcohol vapors, then, bottoms up. The alcohol goes straight to the brain and they "fly." You have to watch them a bit and not serve them too quickly otherwise you lose them too fast. It can be a bit annoying "the hand"; you don't always remain intact. It's no longer exactly the "crazy hand" that we were doing in the '90s. We invented it because we thought it was funny but it was too dangerous. Now it's a bit more of a developed product.

I sometimes call Patrick at Le Bar around midnight from Lausanne to know how he is, he has no mobile phone so Tuesday is usually good because there are not so many clients: one or two tables maximum, and he closes early, around 2 or 3 a.m. Sunday and Monday you can't reach him, he's in the Val d'Oise checking his accounts. I can hardly imagine him out of Le Bar.

Le Bar is invisible from the street. No sign, just an inscription on the doorstep where you can read: Tes Yeux. Patrick opens the door with a button situated under the counter. He accepts everyone—well it depends if it's the right moment or not. The walls are covered with black velvet curtains, the front window on the street side too, the architecture is an L shape, at the bottom, a tunnel without light, you have to bend down to stand, you don't know when it stops, it looks like it would go on forever. The used sofas made with "skaï" have been here for decades. The Asian decoration was here before Patrick. If you want to change the decoration, you need to have a better idea.

What has changed according to him is not the inside of the bar but the outside: the street and the weather. Well actually, yes, there is no smoking inside anymore. You have to smoke outside. And not to make noise. Not to talk. To be quiet. Several times the police came because of the neighbors' complaints. Patrick already got three warnings.

As the taxi driver says: Patrick, he's a good guy, and Patrick's clients are good guys, you can trust them. Going out of the car, AnnE wants to pay and asks him for a "fracture."

She asks for a "fracture" instead of a "facture" (a receipt): it's not a slip since she doesn't know the meaning of the word fracture. She's lived in Paris for a year and has just started learning French. For a year she's also practiced French boxing (*savate*) in a club between

Place de la République and Gare de l'Est. Ibrahim teaches there; he's a world champion of French boxing and Vovinam. He travels from Sarcelles several times a week, AnnE from the city center at the Cité des Arts where she lives. AnneE brings me to the boxing lesson during the summer. We've worked together for several months. Then, I bring Anne. I write everyday to Anina who is spending a few months in the United States. Everyday we meet at la Terrasse des Archives, Catherine's "office" with the group, whose constellation varies depending on the availability of each of us.

The first class: I get changed in the dressing room and enter the boxing room where I see AnnE. People stare at me with funny faces. Someone bursts out in laughter because apparently, due to my unfamiliarity with these clothes, I mistook the boxer bra for the final uniform, when in fact you have to add a t-shirt on top of it. I go back into the dressing room and come back with a t-shirt on. First lesson by Ibrahim: you shouldn't be afraid of getting hit. But then you have to hit. The boxing has a strange effect on me: it makes me cry. So in the dressing room after the lesson, teardrops appear. AnnE joins me and confesses that boxing has had the same effect on her. Second lesson, still with Ibrahim: demonstrations against the bombings in Gaza are happening on la Place de la République. The atmosphere is tight; the first demonstration had been forbidden. Hundreds of CRS are surrounding the place in battle gear; it's been like this for several days. Ibrahim tells me that television teams try to interview the children that he is taking care of in Sarcelles, because they think there are tensions in that neighborhood. He told them to go away. Then he teaches us how to bind our hands. The fingers must be well-separated when you bind the phalanges. Then how to wear the gloves. The strong foot and fight must be "en réserve." You defend yourself with your weak side to fight better with your stronger side. The body has to get used to doing things in reverse. It's not easy, apparently I have a crazy leg, as Ibrahim calls it: my leg always wants to step forward instead of staying backward. Nevertheless the body learns quickly, and after two hours of training, the crazy leg remains where it should be. Tears rise. I fight with AnnE. She moves slower and measures her strength. I move myself a bit in any direction, as if I were miming the fight, most probably because of the timidity provoked by this new situation. You don't know how to behave, where to stand in the room, who's looking and how, how to use the material. I continue miming. AnnE is really fighting, for me, it will come in the third lesson: how to learn to really move with your fights and your feet. To protect your face and to dodge. A kick in the pants, the seat: I accidently give one to Ibrahim, of course it's forbidden by the rules. You fight an opponent of the same weight. You can use the hands and the feet. You need at least one "fouetté" (lateral kick) during a round, which lasts one minute and thirty seconds, then one minute of rest. Three rounds for a match. Kicks in the tibia are forbidden. The attack ensues with hits to the face, frontals and laterals, above the belt, avoiding the breasts for women.

We go drink a coffee after the lessons. Ibrahim, who trains us, does not drink because he is observing Ramadan. He's lost weight, around five kilos. The normal regime starts again tomorrow, he's not so sure, it depends on the moon's position. The following lessons with Anne: we use punching bags and jump ropes, we also train by kicking against piles of recovered mattresses, first battle in the ring with strangers: we learn how to control our strength and our gestures, sweating, we start to realize our own strength and that of our opponent. The room is generally silent; you hear the kicks and sometimes music. A battle with Anne, I'm afraid of hurting her. I often stop my kicks half way. Battle one on one, the referee controls the rules, the ring is delimited by ropes. I continue to follow Ibrahim's teaching. After several weeks I start to get myself used to it and my body changes, the muscles are more visible. The boxing is hand-to-hand fighting. Violence is physical and direct. You are not used to it. You are alone with yourself and your opponent, who reflects your image. Strengths and weaknesses must be managed immediately; the emotions must also be confronted directly. You win a match in your head. You have to convince your partner that you are stronger. Cunning in relation to your opponent, dissuasion strategies. Not showing anything, even if you suffer or you're hurt. Pretending not to be hurt. So he will doubt. You have to either dissuade the opponent or intensify. Not being transparent, not letting them see through you. For Ibrahim, violence is easier to manage on a ring than on the street: it is where you have to free your violence if you want to fight the other to the KO. Ibrahim started boxing when he was 13. You can continue all your life but you have to be careful with kicks to the head. One of his friends doesn't have clear ideas anymore. He had taken too many kicks; some people come to boxing only to get hit.

The discipline rapidly changes into a habit. The body gets used to it very easily, and soon, if you don't train, things get worse. Actually AnnE went to buy a kicking bag this afternoon. She doesn't want to stop training and is worried about not being able to bear the summer break.

Ibrahim knows how to read bodies, he sees everything and also knows how to keep what he sees for himself. That's why I trust him. The direct physical relation of boxing is managed by a control of distance and by a balance of force. It is about a control that one imposes on oneself and the other in the instant exchange with the opponent. Ibrahim sits in front of me at the table in a coffee place, he is a bit curled up, which is also the defensive position, but he constantly looks at the floor because he is not at ease. We speak the same language but we don't always understand each other. I see myself in his eyes, he probably in mine, which does nothing to put either of us at ease. Our habits are like a third person is seated with us at the table. We are both attentive not to register it too much in order not to put the other in an awkward position. He has worn his glasses. That evening, I go back home to République and watch two movies:

La Maîtresse (1976), Bulle Ogier: "I love him because he is the only man I don't distrust." The actress climbs up the stairs of the dungeon with difficulty. She is suffocating, can't breathe anymore, she thinks it is her dominatrix corset that is too tight but it is an anxiety crisis.

Holy Motors (2012), minute 63:55: "I'm afraid of the cameras. They used to be heavier than us; today they have became smaller than our heads."

When I trip on a pile in the street, I feel ashamed before it hurts. I wonder if the people there have seen me. Every day for the last 10 years, Romain walks from rue Vaugirard to the Boulevard Saint-Germain to go to the *tabac*. He knows the way so well that he can go out without his cane. He drinks a coffee a bit further on the Boulevard. Then to rue de Condé to buy bread, passing by rue de l'Ecole Polytechnique. He asks me what I look like. I start to laugh. He starts to laugh too. It's a bit embarrassing. I think a few minutes; I don't know where to start. Long hair, brown eyes, spotted with beauty spots, a bump on the nose, very white skin, an asymmetrical mouth, strange teeth, not very tall, thin and muscled. He never thinks about how people look. One morning, he decides to go all the way to the end of the street after the *tabac* and realizes that the *tabac* is, in fact, next to the bakery, just 50 meters away: he never thought about it. It is at this moment, when he links the two streets to each other, that he decides not to choose between his jobs as a writer and a pianist. He will do both. He hesitated for a long time during his studies at Sciences Po; he needed something that could make him travel while staying in the same place. I ask him if, when he travels, he uses the accents to imagine the landscapes, he says he speaks bad English and this complicates everything a bit, he has a problem making himself understood. He thinks I am 31 years old: 31 for my self-assurance, not more, because of my enthusiasm and my hopefulness. He manages to guess gender thanks to the voice, excluding children before the age of 5.

In the subway in London, I look at the posters glued in fake golden frames on white tiles "Tell us what you think." The same in Paris two hours later, an advertisement by SNCF: "Switzerland is next door: Paris-Lausanne: 25 euros." I get on the train and it stops between two stations. I feel once more that a claustrophobia crisis is arising. I adopt one of my most efficient strategies: the ignorance system. To ignore one's own environment in order to take the anxiety level down, so that the crisis doesn't blow up. I look at photos on my mobile phone to forget where I am.

2.

An afternoon of extreme heat with Marie, we decide to spend our time at the swimming pool in Brooklyn. In the apartment, before we go out, Marie asks me to show her my swimsuit; I think this question is a bit weird but I show it to her. Her answer surprises me even more: she says it should be ok.

I really didn't get why she was asking me to show her my swimsuit. At first I thought it was just out of curiosity but it was something else, because then she asked me to show her my towel too. The swimsuit shouldn't be a problem she says but the towel might be a bit more complicated. It might not be accepted. I ask her to repeat the question, thinking I've misunderstood.

Misunderstandings often happen between us because of our specific accents coming from two different mother tongues. Mine is of course stronger because I've just arrived. Marie has lived here 4 years now. She explains to me that the swimming pool has a very strict policy. They only accept specific models of swimsuits and towels otherwise you just can't go in. We arrive close to the swimming pool: there are 500 meters of metal fences installed to contain the crowd that we have to follow before getting in. We walk this path even though no one is there at this time of the afternoon. There, we have to pass through a first security check: a man controls if we have our locks. Without a lock you can't go in. Then we go to the dressing rooms. After having changed cloths and put on our swimsuits, we arrive at another security checkpoint. Two women are standing at the dressing room exit, they point their fingers towards the showers and then to a sign where we can read: "shower obligatory."

It is indeed obligatory, otherwise impossible to reach the pool area. After having taken a shower, we reach the final control, the one for the swimsuits and the towels. First they check the swimsuits—it seems to be ok—then they ask us to open our towels to see if nothing is hidden inside. They look for weapons and mobile phones or any items which can take photos: they are forbidden in the swimming pool area. So we open our towels and it's all clear. They say our slippers are not 100% ok. My towel seems to be a problem as well. Marie looks at me and I can read on her face that she is a bit worried. But she tells me that it's going to be fine. A woman standing next to us starts to speak to me: "You know you have all kind of religions, sexual orientations and origins in there—it's mixed—so they have to be really careful that no one feels offended because tensions can rise fast when it's all mixed. Usually everything works out good but I heard that there have been problems in the past." Probably because people are almost naked here, it seems to be a bit more tricky than on the subway.

The two guards start to scream at us "Where are your slippers?! Show us! Those slippers are not allowed here! You have to go change! You have to take a regular towel. No! This is not a towel. This is a sheet! You can't enter with this! Have you closed your lockers with a key? It's obligatory! Let me check your towel. This is NOT permitted here! THIS is a sheet! THIS IS NOT A TOWEL!" So Marie's worries are confirmed. Our slippers are accepted, finally, even if they are not totally according to the rules, but I can't come in with my towel. I bought this towel in India, it's hand woven and looks really nice, white with two thin red stripes, woven so fine that it's almost transparent, the classic Indian towel. But here it seems that this towel is a sheet. Luckily, Marie anticipated the problem and took a second terry towel for me just in case.

Later Nora comes to dinner at Marie's place. I've been living together with Marie for a month now. I will cook a pot-au-feu. Not easy to find the right ingredients though. The meat that I bought isn't what it looks like. It's not a roast but a flat steak rolled as if it were a roast. So when I open the plastic, the meat opens itself wide and flat on the table. I hope it will be fine too. Let's try. Anyway there are no other options.

Nora has also just arrived in New York. She needs to rent a van for a transport, and doesn't know how to do it. First a car company told her that she couldn't rent a van because she doesn't have an international driving license. I think it's not true since I did it myself with a Swiss driving license last year in Texas. Marie tells her that a friend knows a place. The thing with New York is that everything is complicated, but you have to ask. You shouldn't be afraid to ask for a favor, this European thing, as a European it's hard because you don't like to ask. You're always afraid of asking for money too. But here everyone is so used to it. And people are used to being asked and to talk about money! You have to ask and talk about money otherwise people think you're stupid and they try to take advantage of you. Make it simple and clear. People here don't like messiness and confusion, which is typically European. It's the most capitalist country and we are in the most capitalist city. It's a trade system clearly run by money, which makes everything really clear.

Nora is a bit afraid of driving in New York. Driving in a foreign city is always frightening the first time, but in New York, I personally love it. The way the streets are built, this grid system, it makes everything really clear and easy, I felt good and reassured even the first time, you have large perspectives and it's impossible to get lost. Nora just had her visa accepted and that's also why she's a bit afraid of renting a car now. It's always complicated. She also needs to open a bank account. First she goes to Chase but Chase doesn't want her. She brings her security number, her visa, but they need a letter from her employer with her address and how much money she earns, none of which she can provide, plus they charge 12 dollars per month. And they are like: but you will maybe succeed, with us, and you have a great network, and maybe your situation will improve in the future! She leaves to go to Santander because she also wants to support this company. But they say that she has to pay every time she gets money. Finally she goes to Citibank and they open an account for her immediately. She accepts even if she has to pay something every month since it's a cheaper deal. Nora explains to the guy at Citibank that she was already a Citibank client before, in Germany, but then this other bank swallowed Citibank. The bank guy says: you could still come back to the family! So at least now she has a bank account, she has just a debit card, a social security number, and a visa so she can work. Then she changes her iTunes to an American account so she has other options for films and music. Much better options. When you link your iTunes to an American Bank account you have a totally different range of everything.

Marie downloads everything illegally. *Pirate Bay*. She's done that since she was a teenager living in Sweden, over 10 years ago. For all the programs, she goes on *Pirate Bay* and she cracks the code. But Germany is crazy, a friend of Nora's was caught for watching a bad movie. They can delete things on your computer. They are so formal. It's all about formalism in Germany. Marie explains that another solution is to use *Little Snitch*. And it's so fun to crack codes! You go into this other dimension of the software programs. You just understand better how they are done. Most people have no idea of how it works. You need to be offline when you do this. But it's not that difficult. You just have to not be afraid, look at the tools and use them. It's like making art. If you see how art is made, you just have to dare to do it. Nora also has to find a new flat soon. Well basically you have two kinds of people: the ones that have to work all day to pay their rent, and the ones that own real estate. Today real estate is a very good and safe investment. The other solution is to sublet your flat if you live in an attractive city. So in 5 days you can usually make back all the rent you have to pay in a month. It's a kind of a job too. You have to manage the organization, clean the flat and the sheets, those kinds of things. That's what Marie does. So she can be free with her time, and do what she wants. It's also a good way to share a bit of the profit with her landlord. We eat the pot-au-feu, it tastes the same but also different because of the flat meat.

Oh I love your style! Later Marie introduces me to Juliana at 11:11, and we immediately get along: I love your style, it's so cruise!

I'm wearing more or less the same clothes I've worn since I was 10, I chose my haircut when I was 7. Juliana has long dark brown braids that match with her skin, they fall around her body down to the knees. She changes her haircut almost everyday but the long braids coiled in a snail shape on top of her head are what I prefer. She is tall and thin, wears platform shoes, has a beautiful, rather deep voice because she was born both male and female. She has always decided very precisely what she wants to wear. She invents herself a new character almost every week, and it's become her work. She's an artist, a performer, a writer, never went to an art school, and the first Friday night of the month, she DJs at 11:11, a club in a bar's cellar, hidden behind a door dressed up as a pile of boxes. It's always really warm there, with lasers projecting all kinds of patterns on the crowd. You can dance, drink and smoke in that cellar. That evening there was such a lack of oxygen that my lighter's flame couldn't burn. It would just extinguish instantly every time I lit it. The lack of oxygen becomes more and more intense and I start to have problems breathing. I look at the door and think: that's it, if I pass out here, I'll stay forever with this crowd dancing on my body, I'll never manage to go out. But this doesn't really matter since Juliana's music is so good. I think it's because she's in a really good mood. She tells me that she's just found a sponsor for her makeup. It costs her a lot of money since she often paints entire parts of her body. Tonight she has blue pearl lips and one green arm. Here everyone has a style: you have to have one. You see all kinds of styles when you walk down the streets, it's really funny, people make comments on each other's style all day, especially in the subway.

I'd bought cheese in the mountains just before coming to America, so a few weeks later Marie and I organize a fondue dinner. I find the longer forks that I need pretty easily. No one has eaten this dish before. The dinner is going well until one of the guests vomits all over the table.

He couldn't hold it. In the middle of a sentence, vomit sprays out of his mouth and spreads out all over the table, over the phones and the guests. He's been a vegetarian since forever; his stomach must be a bit more sensitive. Apparently this happened to him once as a child: his parents forced him to eat a steak. He just couldn't bear it.

At the airport my flight is among the last ones to leave before the storm. The haze is now so dense and it's so foggy that it's impossible to see what's happening outside. They say it will be the worst storm ever to hit the city. The airport is empty and about to be shut down. It's really quiet, as it probably must have been here during the final decades of the last century. What happened in Paris last week doesn't seem to have made any impact: the guards are relaxed. The only new protocol is the one with the kind of vacuum cleaner looking for forbidden particles on your hands, but this had already started a few months ago. The plane is taking off. Luckily I get the last aisle seat. I have no screen in front of me because I sit near the emergency exit but it's ok, I will just open my computer so I can look at something and I also feel reassured by the *wifi* connection and battery plugs situated under my seat. The *wifi* on the plane: I never had this before. I'm chatting with AnnE up in the air. It seems strange. The flight is quiet and we don't feel any sign of the approaching storm. I have a sleeping pill with me, I have had it with me for a year now.

I also have Marie's clothes with me. I left her my pants, shoes, jewels, my favorite red suit jacket that my grandmother Malou bought in Deauville a long time ago—the cruise one—and the bracelet with two sea horses embracing each other that Anne gave me. Jean Painlevé, the French scientist, filmmaker, artist and designer made it: he had to stop his jewels production in the 40s because of the war. Marie has chosen three outfits for me that she was wearing last week. When she stops wearing something after an uncertain period of time she can never wear it again. So it has to be the clothes she's wearing now. I'll wear them for a week and she will do the same to see what happens.

3.

Everything is ready to go to the airport: I walk down the street to pick up my car that I parked one block away last night. I've planned five hours to pick up something at Sylvère's, drive to the rental company to return the car, and check in at the terminal. I can't miss this flight otherwise I'll be stuck in LA. I'm staying at Amy's, but she left for Hawaii this morning at six so I'm alone in town. I walk up the block, see my car, go nearer, and realize that it's not it, my eyes have some difficulties recognizing this car that I've only had for a week, I walk around the entire neighborhood: impossible to find it. It's a nightmare, turning around this neighborhood, staring at all those cars; maybe it was not well parked and taken away, maybe there was a sign that I've missed, or another rule that I don't know about; walking up and down every street for hours again and again, pressing the red button on my key; if I don't find it, I'll never be able to leave the city, now all the houses look the same, and I can't find Amy's house anymore: I'm completely lost.

Amy is in Hawaii: she booked an airb&b because it's cheaper, but you have to be on top of it, you have to do it fast, don't wait until the last minute for that, because people snap up the property very quickly, so they are booked very fast. The first day when she checked there were many things, and by the time she decided where to go almost everything was gone. The one she chose was advertised as a Zen retreat, if she would have planned ahead she could maybe have found something else but the plane tickets are so cheap at this time of the year, that's also why she decided to go. She will rent a surfboard there because it's cheaper than taking hers in the plane.

With Amy yesterday, driving to San Onofre Beach: the last California waves before Hawaii. She lives close to the beach but she doesn't go surfing there because it's a harbor so it blocks the waves, three four times a year the waves would go over the wave breakers, it's like a tsunami. She also doesn't go because she thinks the water tastes like metal: America has some dirty parts. The beach she goes to is where the shipping containers boats are. She doesn't eat fish everyday, but her boyfriend's dad likes to fish, he goes on fishing trips with other fishers; they go for about ten days, to Mexico or Costa Rica, staying on the boat the all time, he catches tuna for yellow fin, wahoo, grouper, all different kinds, not swordfish, but fish that you can eat. When they come back they give it to a guy that cuts them and freezes them so it's really fresh, sometimes Amy eats those fish: you know who caught them.

The surfing: it's not complicated. There is a way to do things, at the beginning you just have to do things the same way. First of all, because you are a beach person, you have to live in your car, you have to go back and forth between the beach and the car. The difference between the people that go all the time and the people that only go sometimes is the awareness of keeping a tidy ship: you try to keep everything clean so that when you go in and out of the car you might want to dust your feet, your shoes, your wetsuit, try to change without touching the sand. It takes some time to know how to do it but you learn pretty fast. Amy can change without letting a sand corn go on the wetsuit or in the car.

You can do it your way but it's not sure that you will manage. Because if you're going to the beach everyday your car will be like a sandbox: it's disgusting. So you have to keep it clean because you don't want to be constantly washing your car. Likewise for the surfboard, you have to wash the salt off. Don't put it on the sand when you get out of the water. Some of the beaches have showers so you can also wash it there. You can also wash yourself and the wetsuit, so it will wash the sand but also the salt because salt is very corrosive.

Over time it will eat up things, ruin them, you want to wash the salt off. For the beaches that don't have showers you bring a bottle of water and you pour it on your body to wash yourself. If you go everyday you want to be on top of it, and put suncream on everyday too—you want to be careful with the sun—Amy goes every day but it depends on the weather, sometimes the weather is not good: basically the weather affects the waves, so when the wind is blowing in the wrong direction it can ruin the waves. Wind blowing from the land to ocean is good, wind blowing from ocean to land is not good. You want to wash the surfboard before putting it on the car if you can: when you get out of the water you go straight to the car instead of sitting on the beach in the sand. It's much better and cooler to rinse off the surfboard, put it on the car, or if you know that you are going to surf again, you can put it on the sand, it's fine. But if you don't know whether you are going to surf again, it's just better to wash it and put it on the car. A lot of people that haven't surfed much, they hang out in their wetsuit all day, like they don't take it off ever, they would eat their lunch in their wetsuit: that's poor taste. You get out of your wetsuit, wear a normal outfit, then you eat lunch. If you hang out with your wetsuit all day, it gets gross, it just feels gross, so it's better to not do that if you can, you don't want that: just get out of the suit.

Second thing: when you're carrying the surfboard. This woman for example, she's sort of carrying the surfboard in a good way but sort of not. Usually it's better to carry the surfboard wax down. Never put the wax toward the sun because the sun would melt the wax, and then it would ruin everything. Likewise when you put the surfboard on the beach, you just turn it around. Same thing when carrying the board toward the beach, bottom side up. Ergonomically, it is better to take the curve under your arm, so you carry it that way. The fin in the front is always better than the fin at the back because the fin area is more narrow so you can carry it easier under your arm, unless you're a giant: then you don't care.

Some people like to stretch before going in the water: Amy doesn't really do that. You can do it if you want but she doesn't think it's really important. Once you're in the water, you always want to find the path of least resistance. You want to find the way to swim out into the ocean so that you don't struggle as much. Also, you don't want to struggle against the waves when you're riding them. This is trickier and it might take a longer time to understand. If you grew up next to an ocean maybe it's easier. The waves are like mountains, they look like moving small hills, there is a top part, then the sides, it's like a triangle. The top part is the first to turn into white water, and the first part to break. So if you're going from the land to the ocean, you never want to stay at the top. You always want to go through the valleys. Because that way you don't have to go against the current, you can just slip through, for that you have to zigzag sometimes, you are paddling, and then: oh here, there is a valley! So you take it, you try to trace the valleys all the way through.

A lot of people say even before you start surfing, even before you enter the water: take some time and watch the waves. Study the waves and find the paths, the water is a path, like a hiking trail. For this beach, where she surfs here all the time: she knows the paths. Each beach is different depending on the shape of the bottom, the contour. Amy started surfing when she was a teenager, but not all the time. She only started to go a lot two years ago. You can learn at whatever age. One thing with beginners, they catch a wave when they are not supposed to, or they cut somebody off, you need to break because it can be dangerous, beginners don't have awareness.

Can you float with the wet suit? Not really, but with the leash, your board won't go that far. You just need to pull the leash. Or you swim to the board. Maximum 8-10 feet usually, which is not far. For Amy it was maybe easier because she has good balance and used to swim when she was younger—on a team, serious training—she has the conditioning for surfing, it's natural to her in this way; but it took her a while to be better and she's still learning things. Always remember paths are resistant, meaning: don't fight. Just relax, and follow the same flow as the ocean. If you feel that you're drowning, just float. There is something called the survival float. If you're in a swimming pool and something happens—you feel you can't float because you have a dead arm for example—try to go to the bottom, try to make yourself like a very skinny stick, sink down to the bottom, and when you hit the floor of the swimming pool, jump up: jump as high as you can and scream loud and quick. And up and down, so that you're not using energy, you're just jumping.

In the ocean, what you do for the survival float is to put your face down in the ocean, like a cross, and then you breathe from the sides. When you're in that position you will float and you don't have to work. Your body naturally wants to float. It's just about the position. If you go this way you will sink. If you go that way you will float. So you will go that way. You can float for hours.

With the rip current: never fight against it. Because if you fight it, it's like swimming up a river, you get tired and then you will be in trouble. A lot of people don't know this. Sometimes there is a current that pushes out to sea: don't fight it. Let the current take you away. The thing with the rip current is that it's scary because it keeps pushing you further and further out to sea, but it's going to stop. It will pull you out, and at one point it will just become equalized because when the water is deeper, there is less current. What creates the rip current is when the waves crash: it needs an escape, a way to get out. Otherwise the land will be completely flooded. The triangle: you want to go through the valley, actually you're going through the rip currents, you are using the rip current. Rip currents are scary but when you surf you can use them to help you to go faster. They can take you out but it will stop. When it stops, you are in deeper water, you have to swim parallel to the ocean, then you can go back in with the crashing waves, they will take you in. It's difficult to recognize people in the water, you say hi to a friend and it's not him: that happens often. How you recognize good surfers here at San Onofre: they don't have a leash, they can see the paths, they know where to go.

This guy in the car stopping next to us, he does a weird thing with his beard, we start to stare at him, he notices it, and he stops immediately: it's really bizarre that people can feel when other people look at them, even in two different cars.

I'm still looking for my car, the sun makes me sneeze—I have a sun sensibility—the streets are empty, nobody. I see someone coming out of his house to get in his car, he's in a hurry, can't help me but if he were me—you don't want to lose your car in LA—he would call the police: 911. There is a police vehicle at the corner, a woman sits next to the policeman to report a crime. I have to wait in the back seat, there is no space for my legs and there is no stuffing in the seat, I'm sitting on a black hard molded plastic piece and you can't open the windows. Now I'm stuck in the back seat and it's getting really warm, but my will to find my car and leave this city is stronger. He finally drives me around the block a few times and we find it. I drive fast and manage to go to Sylvère's, then straight to the airport. I still have to return this car but I forgot the address, I see a shuttle bus of my rental company: I follow it and it knows where to go.

4.

The train has just crossed the border. I remember images of the ride twenty years ago, the LED lighting has just been installed in the Swiss wagons and on the train station's information signs didn't yet exist in Italy then; after Lake Geneva is Lake Maggiore, on the other side of the Alps, and today there are strikes in Italy so I'm hoping the train will arrive at *Milano Centrale*, that I will be able to attend this dinner and go home the next day. If I have understood correctly, the strikes are only stopping the regional trains and not the international lines. I'm starting to feel much better when I travel than when I'm at home, it has become the normal state. Not to move and to stay home, that's what is strange now. The body has simply gotten used to being in movement.

Impossible to set myself at the right hour last time I came back from the United States. I left my watch set to New York time for weeks and was falling asleep at impossible hours. It has become complicated to stay more than three days in the same place; every day is a different city—or it is the same city speaking different languages, a new city forming over the old ones—you don't really know anymore. Constantly travelling is like ski touring every day: you have to keep checking your gear to make sure you have everything you need, that you didn't forget anything—most important is the phone.

Sometimes you check twenty times a day to make sure if it is indeed in your pocket. You develop the skill of packing your suitcase in your head at any time of the day or night. You mentally scroll through your wardrobe, then compose outfit combinations following the genre and number of events you will have to attend. From fifteen days and up to one month, you have enough items to make a tour and the suitcase stays the same. The problem is crossing between seasons during the same trip, then it becomes disruptive to think of two moments of the year at the same time, to imagine your entire wardrobe simultaneously and without crossfading. It's like layering two years on top of each other, the past one and the one that's coming.

When I go to Milan by train, I always think of Malou. She was a writer and a translator, and we used to travel this way together in the '80s-'90s, and in the '00s too. We were visiting family, Bruno and her cousin Jacqueline; they grew up like sisters in the '30s. Malou used to tell me that they would "hop their way to school," imitating the maimed, limping war casualties they were seeing everywhere. When Jacqueline died Bruno started to lose his mind: she was the love of his life, they did everything together. In the morning he was still okay, but at night he would mistake me for my mother.

His mother used to visit him from Southern Italy—he would tell this story ten times a day—coming by train with live chickens in cages, which she would store on the balcony and behead for dinner, one after another according to the number of guests. It was delicious. Today this would be forbidden by the health department. In the taxi with Massimiliano, he introduces me to Alberto. I tell them the story of Malou's friend, an editor who decides one day to write his own book. He's in his house in Venice, goes out to buy fancy paper, a feather pen and ink, and when he gets back home he writes his name on the first page, then goes out again to take a walk and falls down dead. Alberto tells me I'm speaking about his grandfather.

My mother spoke Swiss German to me until I was five years old but I've forgotten everything. I could speak Italian but it's a bit remote in my head, I can't really find the words anymore. I'm listening to Liscio, who's sitting next to me at this dinner, and when he speaks Italian I understand everything. He explains that he buys back businesses to help them develop, mostly by exporting themselves. Those enterprises are active in industry, they have a high expansion potential but no vision for that. Most of them are family businesses and have this potential but they just don't even think about it! So Liscio helps them to enlarge their thoughts. He tries whenever possible to keep the same employees in their jobs, as well as the management, which is generally more efficient but not always. Then he adds his knowledge like an additional layer, like frosting on a cake. His own company has seven thousand employees around the world. For the ones he purchases he provides the contacts as well as the knowledge they need so they can increase their market shares by transplanting somewhere else—usually in India and China—depending on what they produce: you have to find the right product for the right place, a product that translates from one culture to another. This would have interested Malou. Then he asks me in English: "So who are you? What's your essence? What's your flavor?"

Coming back from Vietnam, Massimiliano wakes up in the middle of the night and falls off his bed. He took a dive that almost killed him. He'd simply forgotten where he was after having slept in a dozen places over a dozen days, or maybe it was a hallucination due to jetlag sleep which can sometimes create a kind of fever, like a really deep sleep in the afternoon, where it's difficult to distinguish reality from dream.

Born in Bergamo, he now lives between New York and Milan. His work takes him to Hô Chi Minh City and Poland, and he's just decided to rent another flat in Los Angeles. Meanwhile, he's moved his office into a church which is split in two by a wall, creating two mirrored spaces with similar dimensions: one for the cloistered nuns, the other for the public. Behind the church there was once an adjoining convent which disappeared two hundred years ago to make room for buildings. The sisters used to travel between the convent and the church several times a day, their only movements consisting of these back-and-forth walks.

They went back and forth from the convent to the church to attend the mass on the other side of the wall. Cloistered, observing through the iron bars of a small window behind the altar, all they could see were the priest's raised hands as he presented the host during the Eucharist. Upon entering the convent, the young women added the prefix "angelic" to their surname and they had to be silent most of the time. The second half of the church, explains Massimiliano, will remain open to the public: half office, half exhibition space. He wanted to build a structure that didn't damage the original building and was resistant to earthquakes, a kind of boat permanently parked inside the church. The top floor pitches slightly as it spans the wall that splits the church in two, and from up here you can overlook the entire public half. You feel like a captured bird, zooming in on murals painted by the Fratelli Campi four hundred years ago, a slight vertigo feeling.

The church was deconsecrated two hundred years ago. It still belongs to the Vatican, who is Massimiliano's landlord. Signing the contract took seven months to finalize: seven months compared to eternity is not that long. Around 1550, the countess Ludovica Torelli di Guastalla founded the Order of Angelic Sisters, who inhabited the adjoining convent of the Chiesa di San Paolo Converso. It seems she built this place in order to transgress her own rules. Women born in the wrong position were usually placed in a convent against their will so as not to divide the family's fortune. It was a jail made for women you didn't know what to do with. All contacts with the outside was forbidden. The countess's changes consisted in establishing some sort of visiting hours, thereby deregulating love relationships: not a total lock up, offering partial captivity.

Carissa started to have a claustrophobic crisis a year ago. In the subway at rush hour, on her way to the doctor, the train stopped between two stations. Since then she always takes a pill with her, a tranquilizer. For a year she's managed to get along without the pill but she just took one this afternoon when the subway stopped inside a tunnel. It only lasted a minute but for her it was an eternity.

The Northern Line in London is the worst one. You access it by going down a series of four, five, six escalators. It's possible to find alternative paths to avoid this line, but when you don't have a choice you have to take a deep breath and just go. What's particularly horrible, worse than the endlessly swallowing escalators beneath the city, is the train's architecture. This unbearably thin tube becomes a nightmare when it's crowded. One day Stefan tells me that you shouldn't worry, because in case of a problem, there's always a way out the train: you have to push back the doors with your arms very forcefully and walk along the tracks. This may sometimes be the case, but not on the Northern Line.

With Stefan in Wakefield passing by the jail—for life sentences only—we hear prisoners from the outside, and we think about what AnnE would say if she were with us now: "If you don't want to have problems, avoid eye contact." Separated from the men, the Angelic Sisters were locked up in silence within the adjoining convent of La Chiesa di San Paolo Converso, the church of Saint-Paul the converted. The "conversion" is the most difficult position in ski touring because you have to transfer your entire weight from one leg to the other and it's just at that moment that you can lose your balance and fall into the void.

I'm discovering techniques to lessen the crises that threaten to emerge on various occasions: tunnels, subways, planes. The crisis never blows up but the body remembers. The first crisis, some years ago in a minaret in India, the women were given a kind of ugly shapeless coat or apron which we had to wear to cover ourselves: the spiral staircase suddenly seemed endless to me. You always have to be very careful because the crisis can appear when you least expect it. Recently I was a bit annoyed because there were no more aisle seats and the steward made me wait near the door while he found a free seat. I had just bumped into Adam at the Berlin airport. We passed through the security check together and he had his computer controlled, as always, supposedly a random search but we all knew exactly why. Switzerland had just been voting on a new law in order to increase the emigration restrictions and Adam had been thinking seriously about adopting a second nationality: it's a good way to avoid problems and systematic controls. Our planes were taking off three minutes apart, the doors were side by side and we could see each other in the distance on the tarmac before boarding: he was going to Basel, I was going to Paris.

Last week with Anne in New York, we went to Gavin's on Tuesday, Wednesday, Thursday, and Saturday. Always in different places, always in the same city, Uptown, Downtown, Eastside and Westside. An opening and then: the dinner. Apparently he plays an important role, he's feeding us. The food always tastes pretty good, a bit the same but not quite, depending on the target audience, the average age and the neighborhood. So Uptown was really fancy, Downtown West more party and young but a bit linked to the past and faded, which is why the new East space has just opened, like a newborn little brother. Time travel across two decades, traveling through a world that always tastes a bit the same. It's just boring enough to be reassuring. You feel good and at home, but a bit watched. Everybody notices where you sit, with whom you speak. We spent a really nice evening there on Saturday with Loren. Loren's laugh sounds exactly the same as Olivia's. So every time Loren is laughing—and she is laughing all the time—I think for a second that Olivia is sitting next to me. It's really important to leave at the right time, quite early because you're busy. So on Sunday Anne and I drive to Boston.

Back from Boston, we arrive at Ericka's loft where we're staying, right next to the *Manhattan Detention Complex*. You access the place through a series of three long stairways painted green, the upper floors are sinking toward the inside of the building so you have to watch your steps carefully and focus in order to not lose your balance. It's also possible to take the elevator around the corner: you have to stop on the fourth floor, which is in fact the second, climb some stairs in order to arrive at the third, but first you have to walk two blocks through the inside of the building, follow a corridor, an endless, zigzag labyrinth covered in gray carpet. When the gray carpet ends to become green painted wood, you climb one last stairway, then pass through two doors and arrive at the door of the loft. It's huge, and a cube has been built inside to make a small room at the end. Three hundred square meters and only two windows: the first one on the left near the entrance opens onto an airshaft and doesn't really let any light in, the second one is at the very end of the space. All day long, the loft remains in darkness; after a few days, the eyes get used to it. You have to force yourself into a precise daily rhythm, and most of all go out every morning as soon as you wake up so the body understands it's daytime. The light from outside is dazzling after forty-eight hours inside. After thirty years, the entire outside world must dazzle you coming out of this black box.

Construction of the Simplon Tunnel started in 1898, it was inaugurated in 1906, today you cross it in twenty minutes. Watching out the windows—you can't open them anymore—you see that the mountain's rock has been dug by hand with picks. Still complicated to handle: the conditions at the center of the mountain, the heat, and rock so dense that it suddenly becomes sand as soon as you try to dig it, it melts into itself, becomes almost liquid. It took eight years to dig twenty kilometers.

The train comes out of the tunnel creating a weird sensibility to the colors at nightfall, when the public lighting competes with the daylight. I have some difficulty seeing properly, sitting in the wagon lit by LED lights while gazing at the sunset on Lake Maggiore while an advertisement for the World Expo 2015 scrolls simultaneously on about fifty screens on the wagon's ceiling. My vision blurs for a few minutes: "Y aura-t-il encore des fruits et des légumes dans 40 ans? Parmigiano o Sbrinz? E questo il dilemma! 9 Milliarden Menschen in 2050, können wir alle ernähren? Combattere contro le sprechi alimentari! Si, ma come? In the expo the most amazing pavilions! Italy, China, United Arab Emirates, Israel, Estonia, Chile, Austria, Germany, Switzerland, Azerbaijan, Rice, Spices, Cocoa, Cereals & tubers, Coffee, Legumes & fruits, Arid zones, Bio mediterraneum islands & sea. The thematic pavilions! Future food district, Pavilion zero, Biodiversity's park, Children's park, Arts & Foods!"

Having dinner at the *Triennale*, Massimiliano is cooking Pho. He brought the ingredients a few days ago on his way back from Vietnam. The building was built in 1933, Malou went there as a child with Jacqueline, the fascist architecture and the name *Triennale* remained. A building named "every three years." Massimiliano was born on December 6th, the same day as Malou, during the dinner, he explains that the Milan Cathedral was built with marble from a single mountain. The mountain is near Lake Maggiore, you could certainly see it from the train, and today it's in the center of Milan, its roof covered with hundreds of marble figures who watch over the city and must see the planes from a little closer up.

You don't really think about the people in planes. It was strange to imagine Adam in the plane which I could see on the runway taking off just before mine, I was following it with my eyes for a few minutes. Passing somebody you know in a car on the highway: twice this has happened. In the subway it happens more often. Once, Marie was sitting next to me on the same bench, and after two minutes we turned to each other and jumped.

Ski touring with Olivia and Mai-Thu in the Alps, we arrive at the top of a mountain overlooking the entire valley. We can see Lake Geneva; Lake Maggiore must be a bit further off. The weather changes really suddenly at this altitude so we have to hurry back down before the snow gets too soft. Olivia has been mountaineering for years, it allows her to clear her head: always mind your center of balance and move forward very slowly while staying focused. Like Massimiliano, she enjoys high altitudes.

At the Tea Room *Chez Quartier* one afternoon with John and Mai-Thu: she is about to take her driver's license exam and tells us she will practice driving tonight. John says she's right, that it's a good idea to practice on the moon. The acoustics are pretty bad, the neighbors to the right and left are very loud, when Mai- Thu repeats her sentence a second time we understand that flying breads are driving cars in *apesanteur de lune*. In the plane, on the last day of the year, I had just come down from the Alps, which I saw once again after take-off. Passing over the mountain range, the plane continuing its ascent, I saw Australia, Japan, Vietnam, India, all of Asia, Africa, then Europe changing years on my screen. I think about John and Mai-Thu and try to see the flying breads from the porthole. I look around me and can't help seeing the passengers as different kinds of bread: French baguettes, German Vollkornbrot, Swiss rye bread, New Yorker bagels, Jewish braids.

John has always worn his hair in a long braid which he ties in two places, at the top and the bottom. He hasn't cut his hair for several decades. He says he once went diving in the sea with Olivier whose long gray beard, floating weightless in the water, surrounded him like jellyfish tentacles. John's braid was floating too. They are now waiting in a hotel lobby for Genesis before going out to dinner. Genesis has long blond hair and walks with a stick from Benin. The *Pandrogyne* project, a fusion between Genesis and Lady Jay, began a few years ago: they wanted to become one person. After several operations, the face and body have completely changed. Genesis's old friends say "he" when they talk about him, more recent friends say "she" when they talk about her, Genesis says "us" instead of I.

Nicolas is talking with Mai-Thu about a trip in India at two thousand meters' altitude in a house perched on a mountaintop. It has been snowing all night and the village has been cut off from the world for two days. She notices that Corinna Bille once lived in a chalet not so far away, about a hundred years ago. He checks his phone for some good addresses: the problem today is that when you plan your trip too much, you have the feeling that you've already done it. In India it was like this, you've already seen everything in advance in photos, and when you arrive you recognize the hotel, the restaurant, and like a regular you ask for the table at the far left corner of the room because you already know it's the best one.

5.

In Wakefield with Stefan in a cab: the taxi driver tells us that he
doesn't work at night anymore. He leaves this to the Blacks and the
Arabs, they're the last ones to arrive, it's normal. On tour with *Solar
Lice*, we've been here for ten days, in this old mine city that is completely ravaged, that has been transformed into a domicile for
prisoners and disabled people. Artists are invited here by a new
museum that was constructed to revive the economy of the city. We
are rehearsing with the band in a building recently built for offices
nearby the museum, it is part of an important real estate project: a
new neighborhood.

The giant hall must look like the *Messe* between two fairs, the
building has been completely empty for the last two years, we can
change floors many times a day to install our temporary studio, a
metal floor, white walls, hundreds of neon lights on the ceiling, that
are all linked to one switch: thousands of square meters per floor
that have been thought "open space" style. Every evening, we go
back to the flat that has been put at our disposal: it's a flat for disabled people, it is used by the museum to house artists since the
state is only funding buildings that are disabled friendly. The bath-
rooms are big, bigger than the rooms, and are equipped with
handrails; you can hang on them under the shower, or when you

brush your teeth, sitting on the elevated toilets, your feet are swinging into the void, next to the bed, several alarm strings of different colors. You pull them by reflex sometimes in the morning when you wake up: a nurse's voice comes out from an interphone and asks if everything is all right, if you need help, if the central dispatcher needs to send an ambulance. It can all be so reassuring. In the living room, the sofa's feet have been put on four plastic dog's plates to raise it by a few centimeters to meet the regulatory height. Washing the dishes, I put my plate to the left of the drain like usual, and it falls off, about forty centimeters down into a second sink. It's exactly the same sink, but built twice as low.

On the evening of the fifth day, we finally find a Greek restaurant where we like the food, and decide to go back there for lunch the day after: we don't recognize the place and go out thinking we've switched it with another one. We make a tour of the neighborhood and end up in exactly the same place, same number: it's an English tea-room. It looks like the Greek one but the atmosphere doesn't look the same, the sign, the decoration has slightly changed, the lighting is stronger, it is not the same clientele, some of the employees we met yesterday are mixed with new ones, the menu is different. The boss explains to us that during the day it's an English tea-room, and in the evening a Greek restaurant, so we decide to stay there, waiting for the evening.

Lo-Shen has just opened a wine bar in Bordeaux with her husband. She has been living in France for five years. She changed the entire decoration two weeks ago so that it looks a bit more like a French "bar à vin." Before, it was too much of a normal café style. When I ask her where she comes from, she is at first offended. It's often the case in Europe: people act like they have been here since forever. I tell her that I can't say where her accent comes from but that her French is really good, she answers that she doesn't like being asked where she comes from because she would like to look French, but that she's born in Beijing. In China she used to do dancing, music, and she didn't have the feeling that she was forbidden to do anything, even if it was always very academic, you wouldn't learn to be creative, for example. Even though she has married a European. Her parents never had the chance to discover Europe, but neither her parents nor her grandparents ever felt stifled. The Europeans or the Americans, they think the Chinese are stifled, but if we're happy, well it's fine! She knows that there is some stuff that you can do here that you can't do in China; people are weirder here, not politically but mentally, culturally, really weirder, more original. Many people think that in China people are stifled because of the politics but she doesn't think it's because of this. For five thousand years, it has always been like that. You don't talk about intimate subjects. Even with your best friend, you don't talk about it: sex, never. She was first shocked when she arrived, people talking about sex like snack food. She lives in France; she has always thought that she had a French side. She accepts many things of the French culture, even the jokes on sex. Her parents even told her that she should go some-where else, because she wasn't a real Chinese. At school she wasn't brave. She used to do trashy things, hang out with boys, and that wasn't possible in China, so she wasn't accepted, she was considered a bad girl. One day, for example, she had her ears pierced, and that was forbidden. She hid it under her hair, but her mother caught her; her teacher then told her mother she had to move because she would be unhappy in China. In France, she found herself. In China, it's very stressful, you work the human relationships, the gift's code. No one tells you, no one teaches you, but you have to understand: the "under-table" rules, that's how they're called in China. Chinese people are very shy. You're never told things to your face but you still have to understand, and she just couldn't do that. Her two best friends are in New York and Chicago; over there, it's very simple to meet people. In China, it works between families, childhood friends, neighbors: then you can have a hundred percent trust. Then in life, it's more about meeting people by interest. You meet people with a very precise goal: a business relationship. Her mother's boss, for example—now she's retired, it's at 55 years-old for women, 50 for dangerous jobs—she has been working in a factory, and managed, through her relations, to change her file into the "dangerous job" category. Since then, she goes to see her boss every year. If you have helped someone once, they will thank you all your life. And on top of that, you have many other "under-table" things.

Her knowledge is more of the middle class, the Beijing middle class. She is a single child. This rule, it was only the cities in the '80s, in the countryside, it was that you would sell or kill the young girls, it happened once in one of her cousins' families. Today, you can have two. Before you could have two but you had to pay, you would lose your job, so it was only for the very rich people. Today, single children can have two children: one of the two parents has to be a single child, then you can have a second. But still it's very expensive. Her parents made the calculation: they paid a minimum of fifty thousand euros for her, if you calculate from her birth, that's what she has cost. Even if they had wanted, they would never have been able to afford a second child. But they still have brothers and sisters, so she has cousins that she would call brothers and sisters. The Chinese family: every day, you're surrounded by your family. In France it's not like that. Now she's very far from her parents, her father calls her to tell her that he misses her, and asks her to send pictures. She goes back with her husband once a year—her husband is like their son, even if he doesn't speak one word of Chinese—the world is small but it's still expensive, and ten hours on a plane is long. In the winter it's okay, but in the summer it's very expensive. Well, now they are trying to have a child, it's been two months that she's waiting and she's fed up, she even started to have small pimples because she's so stressed. She looks on the internet for how to get pregnant, some tricks, even if, of course, she knows how to get pregnant! If she gets pregnant, she won't be able to go back home for two years because she won't be allowed to take the plane. She will stay in Bordeaux in her bar with her husband, they have a really good relationship with their business partners, the winemakers, she even sometimes organizes tours of the vineyard for Chinese groups, so they would just stay there and take care of the "bar à vin."

Noé doesn't like to stress for useless reasons, I can go visit him anytime I want at the vineyard, I don't need to call, like Patrick at le Bar, he's always there. The wine estate *Le Satyre* was founded in the 40s by his father. Noé took it over in the '70s. The transition was made in several steps: at University, he chose law, because it was what François, his cousin and best friend was doing, but he also could have done something else, it didn't really matter. He just wanted to go away and do something that would give him a wide array of possibilities after. It's at this moment that he started to get into politics. He entered the POP in Nyon and François took part in the creation of the Lausannoise section of the Ligue Marxiste Révolutionnaire. They met Bernard, with whom they carried out several actions in the '60s: they are the ones that hung a Vietnamese flag on Notre-Dame in Paris during the Têt offensive. They had been hiding in the cathedral when the doors were closing. Bernard, a very good alpinist, climbed there, rappelling; Noé was keeping up the guard. They saw themselves on television the day after: the flag was still hanging, the firemen needed several days to take it down. On the TV news, they were also talking about the fake bomb they had built to slow down the police so the flag could be visible a bit longer.

After his studies, Noé went back to the wine estate and his father gave it to him. He was proud that his son had studied. Noé is still into politics, he is a member of several syndicates in Switzerland and in Spain. Back when the frontiers were closed, it was easier to ship out the production—it's still sixty thousand bottles a year—so before, when you had something left at the end, you just had to make a few phone calls, and everything was sold. Today, it not only needs to be very good, but you also have to seek out a bit. For now everything goes really well: he would sell everything in the wine estate, he can sell everything without moving too much, but you have to watch out a bit, be attentive, go out a bit. He sells half to restaurants, half to private clients; he produces not too much compared to the surface units, and doesn't do promotion.

Noé and his father fought a lot in the beginning: Noé was with the POP, his father with the liberals, but the last twenty-five years, it was "billard." They never made accounts, his father sold him the estate for one symbolic franc and the deal was done. He would give him his bills, and Noé would pay all his costs. You need to work a lot and have a modest lifestyle, once you have a roof over your head, the rest you don't really care about. He thinks that he didn't make many changes compared to his father, that his involvement in politics didn't have that much influence but still. The seasonal workers were badly housed; he used all the profits to build them better houses; to improve cultural life; the working conditions outside were also improved by elevating the vineyards a bit, so they wouldn't need to kneel so much anymore.

He also made modifications in the cellar to improve the working conditions and didn't keep anything for himself; he is well housed, has a view on the lake, lives off retirement pension and that's also a great comfort because he doesn't have anything. And above all no useless ideas. His friends are made, his Spanish colleagues welcome him well: you can't trade this kind of relationship. The restaurant, forget about it. The guys say: but we don't see you! And he answers: I like you, it's nice to see you, but you just have to come to the estate. It's not his thing to play the fool.

Politics is network: you know one, you know a hundred and twenty. It allows you to meet people. It has allowed him to meet people like Morales, Ben Bella, Ziegler—even Dutoit the orchestra conductor passed by the other day. But this is a family network. He's part of these political networks, but withholding. He doesn't go to all the meetings because it's a bit annoying, but he keeps very good personal relationships. It's a network, each one his own. You have to find your register and not force your talent.

You have to go where you feel good. His father was good in the *bistrots*, paying rounds, making jokes; but he can't do that, he would be ridiculous. You have to find your thing, what belongs to your nature, force yourself a bit but not too much. If you're at home alone, first you annoy yourself, you don't discover that much, and life becomes fast and a bit boring. You have to go out, but find the right road. It allows you to build your life somewhere else, not to stick to these things, when people are dead they're dead.

In the '60s, they would go to Paris, also once to Moscow, to see. Paris: if you don't have money you're a piece of shit, and people are racist, aggressive. Noé's father was a violent person, an alcoholic. When Noé was a teenager, they would get in trouble all the time. The ambiance was rotten, his father would shout at him all day long, and if François wouldn't have come to get him out of this, to go study law, Noé would probably have committed suicide. Since the proposition was coming from François, it could only be good. It allowed him to leave this rotten ambiance and to do something else. The studies also allowed him to build a political network. It was both good and bad; there are many douchebags there as well. But it was a way to do something else. If François would have told him, let's enroll in the "légion étrangère," he would have done the same. He just wanted to escape, and François was smart and he had a brilliant idea, because there was the departure, but also elegance: everybody was at the end proud that he was studying. It would break the conflict and take a positive turn. François came one day and said: you get out of here, you leave all this and you come with me. Once the studies were finished, it was done. Because his father was retiring, he was happy that his son would take over the vineyard, and Noé was happy to have seen something else and stand up to his father. He owns François part of his life.

They used to see each other once a week. A meeting like that, every week, he passed by his office, they would go to the gym, then eat something, chat about politics and other stuff. That was one of the great pleasures of life. Noé stopped going to the gym when François died. It does nothing to try to keep things up. Today he does boxing, he is seventy and very few can beat him at jumping rope. But studying, that was François's idea; to break the conflict, but with elegance, without hurting anyone.

6.

I've met Peter several times, always in a different city, always at an opening. At first we looked at each other with some insistence, not being sure if either of us recognized the other person although we knew we'd seen them before. Then he said Hi to me—I must say that I had absolutely no idea where and in which circumstances we'd met. I've since recognized him in pictures that I'd taken in the restaurant in Basel. I remember having talked with him several times, but not in which language we'd spoken. German, English, French; impossible to tell. He lives in Brussels I think, has a German name, and since everyone speaks English it could have been all three. I distinctly remember what we've spoken about every time: about modes of greeting—kissing, shaking hands, different hugging techniques—and about how children kiss, in a somewhat awkward way. And yet it is impossible to tell in which language we've exchanged these words. When I think about certain people, I hear their voice. When I read their messages too. Here, in the case of Peter, I hear absolutely nothing, silence.

When I think about John, I hear his voice, but only the words he tells me in French. His accent is incredible. As for the rest of our conversations, it's hard to tell what we've been talking about. Last time we saw each other, I couldn't stop talking, in English. I don't always really realize what I say in a foreign language; I sometimes wonder about what I say, but mostly about what he hears. Talking about my alpine ski trips in the mountains "en peau de phoque" he understood "I do butt fuck it's really fun." I can still hear the sound of his voice as I was trying to pronounce the word "leather" and couldn't. He said "ta peau c'est du cuir" or "ta peau elle sent le cuir." I didn't understand very well and didn't want to make him repeat a third time. I was so surprised, his voice in French, it was magnificent. Then about Sylvère and his career choice—he likes Sylvère a lot "mais c'est ma malédiction."

John has learned French reading many books over many years. After a while, he started to understand, but can hardly speak it. During a conversation filmed by Sylvère in the '80s in his loft for *Violent Femmes*, Catherine Robbe-Grillet asks Mlle Victoire how to say "se masturber" in English:

"To jerk off."

"Ah jerk off, jerk off... c'est drôle de manipuler des mots qui ne sont rien pour moi. Absolument rien. Je peux le dire, ce n'est pas cru, ce n'est pas obscène, c'est rien... Jerk, jerk... Jerk off... Non ça ne me fait rien du tout."

Then John is nineteen. He has just arrived in New York. He is in college, and Sylvère is his comparative literature teacher. Sylvère hires him as an intern. This first job consists of transcribing tape recordings of sexual deviants. Barely finished with school and having just arrived in New York, John listens for hours to perverts recording themselves describing their own fantasies while masturbating; this is an experiment to test a new kind of cure to heal deviance, to observe the level of the subjects' arousal. You could observe their responses to certain types of images by measuring their penis size, the quality of their erection, and the size of their eyeballs. As if dazzled by a flash, the pupils dilate and reflect the subject's sexual excitement. John is in charge of transcribing all these observations for the book on which Sylvère is working: *Overexposed.*

A flasher recording himself narrating his fantasies over and over, hoping to get bored of his own perversion... The perverts have the choice between two options, either to go to jail or to try this new cure: they have to present their recordings to the doctor at regular intervals, and they are cheating, recording fake fantasies, faking masturbation, faking orgasm, and so faking their healing.

After his studies, John starts working in the cinema industry, but he very quickly grows bored, spending his days waiting. He wishes things were cheaper and simpler, so he decides to open a gallery: it's simpler because you can just think of something and make it happen immediately. He wants to stay independent so that he can work at his own rhythm. Today the situation is different. Back then, the idea was to have a space where you could create your own time, working slowly, but that's not really possible anymore, things move faster, there is more competition, the relation to money is different, people think about money all the time and operate at a higher speed, faster, more professionally, more aggressively. John has tried running on a treadmill at the gym for a while but pretty quickly stopped. Walking is his favorite sport, walking on the street, and every day he crosses the bridge on foot to go to work. That's where you have the best ideas. Walking on the street and rowing alone through the bay in a long oar boat, you are light and fast, it's calm and silent. He has tried to teach for a few years, his students were already professionals: ready to leave school and become rich immediately. *Overexposed* was published in 1987. A pervert recording himself as a new technology, that was something special. Today everyone does it, while making sure to integrate it into their process of professionalism, a very efficient tool used on social media, self-exhibition.

We meet recently in a coffee shop he has chosen. When I arrive, he says the place is not good enough and takes me to another one. I sit down at a table but he says it isn't working either, so we leave to go look for a third place. We walk down the block and then he takes me back to the first one.

Later, as we were having dinner with his friends, I offered him an organic hand soap. There was some in a big barrel on a shelf behind our table, next to different kinds of soaps: soap from Marseille, body soap, hand soap. Soap for sale in a restaurant, that made me laugh. He pushed down on the pump of the large barrel so I could smell; liquid soap spurted out over his hands and flowed down onto the floor. So I wanted to offer him a bottle of soap, because I remembered the first time that I went to his house, he had a dish brush with a plastic box clipped to the top that you could fill with liquid soap, so that the soap spreads directly into the brush. I'd never seen that before. I ordered the soap like that, in the middle of the dinner: the waiter went hog-wild with the pump, it was dripping on every side, overflowing all over the glass.

I'd given John a first gift a few years before, the first time I saw him, at Le Bar in Paris, a portrait. I was drawing three portraits on postcards, Patrick, Daniel, and the last one, a stranger seated at the other side of the bar. I don't really know why. It was the first time I'd seen him and I never draw: I asked his name, wrote it on the drawing—a cap with a giant visor—and gave it to him.

He takes the soap and after dinner, we go to a bar. Walking on the street, John asks me a number of questions about the people I know, about my friends. We'd been eating with friends of his who have known each other for 25 years. He explains to me that he has only known them for 15 years, and asks me if I think that I will still be friends with Marie in 15 years. I say yes. I find it strange that he asks me all these questions. About Anne, about what she was looking for, then about Catherine. I would prefer if he asked them directly, but maybe this is his journalistic side. Or maybe he thinks that he still has to ace the job interview because I forgot to tell him that I've engaged him. He offered to be my adviser a few months before. His humor convinced me, but mostly I was looking for someone who could understand without needing to speak. It's more efficient, especially when you don't speak the same language.

Sometime last month, we are in his kitchen, I bring him the "Towel Chapter" printed with Tannis at the *Office Depot* on Vine Street in Los Angeles. He helps me correct the translation. I need American ears, to translate the text so that it still sounds French but is understandable in English. We go through his kitchen tools for Marie's birthday dinner: a mixer, a giant bowl, and *cannelés* molds. He has six of them, made of aluminum, he offers them to me: piled, they look like the *Chrysler Building*. As I take one, I remember where I'd seen him for the second or third time. I'd bumped into him looking for my way uptown right after I'd had an attack of claustrophobia in the subway.

The trains are so frequent, so full that they create traffic jams under the earth: hundreds of crowded trains one behind the other, it overflows from every side. The crowds try to exit at the station, the tracks are so full that it's impossible to move, to enter or exit the trains. Mine was stopped forty minutes between two stations: your body temperature rises all of a sudden, your heartbeat accelerates, so does your breathing, you don't have any air, your legs are shaking, you become deaf.

I try to think of something else to convince me that I'm somewhere else. I look at my phone and at all these people around me. I look at their teeth. I think of the "pot-au-feu" dinner with Nora and Marie. Nora was just coming back from the dentist: well, it's all about the teeth. Most Americans have braces. When you're a teenager—and they do that to everyone—they take out your wisdom teeth before they are even formed. Here, it's a class thing with teeth; you can see where people come from. Nora went to the dentist because she wanted to get her teeth cleaned. First they took X-Rays of every tooth. Then they e-mailed them to her. In the end, they said everything was ok, but there was one little thing they wanted to do to her, with antibiotics—here you take antibiotics for everything. Then they were like: "we have to talk about the bleaching." Nora looked at the dentist, and she had teeth as white as snow. As white as cocaine. It was incredible. The problem is that your teeth can become porous with bleaching. Nora smokes, drinks coffee all the time. Whatever, she thought, maybe she should do it.

I like Adam's funny teeth, a bit brown, they look like Samon's, who smokes rolled cigarettes all day long. Anne and I had the same accident as children, we both wear a prosthesis. We have somewhat of an asymmetric upper lip from hiding it growing up, and I got used to putting my hand in front of my mouth over the years when I speak. John does it as well, his teeth are slightly lemon color. Today, you're recommended bleaching sessions to start, or another standard practice: the veneer.

White veneers are set on every tooth so that you can have a presentable smile. It's the same thing they do for nails. This is the soft technique, when you're still lucky and have all your teeth. Then there are implants or rings. This technique is more aggressive for the gums, but in any case, it's still better than dentures. Until the 2000s, bleaching and veneers were mostly recommended when you were working in communication, or were a public person, so today, it's for everyone.

They even talk about it in job interview classes. It is highly recommended to help you find a job. Dan is thirty-seven and has been working in the mobile phone industry for the last ten years. The "red line" that defines his career is difficult to describe in his case: he's passionate, plays music, would like to make a living from it but doesn't manage somehow, so he is angry, can't take criticism, which he always questions and turns back on others. A typical case for Samuel who does job interview coaching. He coaches all kinds of people on very large job panels to speak in public and to learn how to present themselves.

He recommends you start with a two-week intensive coaching. For Dan, it's always the other person's fault if there is a problem, which is kind of a problematic attitude that you would absolutely not mention during a job interview. You have to follow the "red line" in your speech: it's a kind of spinal column, composed of five elements that follow your personality throughout your career and that build a base that is solid and recognizable. Then there are the drawers: they contain all of your experiences, your education, and your family situation. There are hundreds of tricky questions for which you have to be prepared: always give the impression you know, even if you have no idea.

Body language, tone of voice, and breath are analyzed as well. Ali is the father of two children and is looking for a job. His goals for the future are to work in insurance, in the security industry, or for an NGO. At home, he has a box that contains all the negative responses to his applications: a hundred in four months. He thinks that he really needs to do something, and feels bad, above all towards his family. There might be an opportunity in a region where there is an armed conflict, and he's hesitant to say yes. Of course he's afraid—mostly because he has a family—but he really wants to find a job because he has lost his confidence. So he will go there next month. It will give him breathing space, financially, and will be good for his CV. Denise is a good listener and also thinks that she has a high capacity to adapt. She has worked in a laboratory for several years and would like to change for a job that is a bit less lonely, but it's not easy because at her age, you're already old. Forty years for women, fifty for men. According to a study, after a long period of improvement, the situation of women on the job market has deteriorated these last twenty years. It could be because we are in a situation of war.

Situations of violence push the job market into a position of retreat; it would snap shut in order to better protect itself. All these analytical tools come mostly from Canada, from Toronto: what is most important is to know how to evaluate yourself at your true value, auto-evaluation. You need to have a good view of yourself, and mostly to know how to transmit it. A trick that is pretty efficient for training is to talk to yourself in the third person.

Before an interview, it is highly recommended to walk around the building twice to get your marks in this unknown environment, then to watch a bird or a cloud, to think of something for a few minutes, and then to go in. When you're in front of several people, one strategy consists in fixing a neutral point in the center so that everyone feels you're watching them. You must not talk to yourself, but to the other: this technique is called active listening. You need to know how to evaluate yourself and to be conscious of how your behavior will be perceived. For example, someone spills coffee on your trousers: how do you react? This can show whether you know how to deal with a crisis. When you talk, you use your random access memory. It lasts five seconds on average. So your answers need to be short, and you should always finish your sentences. Take maximum thirty seconds to finalize a sentence. When a sentence is set down, never take it back. To negotiate your salary, you need to know how to sell yourself, to be conscious of your own value, and to have a good estimate of what's contained in the negotiation. "Mind mapping" is a good tool: it consists in putting words or ideas in bubbles and visualizing the relations between them. There is software that can help you do your own "mind mapping." *Free Mind* for example is free. Once you have the bubbles or drawers, then you can open or close them, it's exactly like a *PowerPoint* that you would have in your head.

Never have two bubbles open at the same time, and erase your memory regularly. In the story of your life, what matters is not coherence in terms of dates, but in terms of content. You can send a recommendation letter that dates back to 1977, but only if it makes sense in the journey of your life. Often, people don't include what they have done in their country of origin. Ali for example, has a Masters in political science, but doesn't dare say it. He never thought he could aim for a job higher up in the hierarchy, and most of all, he always thought that having this Masters blurs the tracks a bit for his employers.

Never use negative words. It takes four times longer to erase a negative word. Always start with a positive word. Also start with what you would like to do and not what you have done. This shows that you're future-oriented. The passage from school to work is very difficult to negotiate. You have to speak about ongoing training: a person who doesn't train is a person who is losing. Any training is good, whatever it is, because it means that you "enable yourself," and that you know how to question yourself. Since September 11th, we can observe two tendencies: the fast doing that generates immediate profit, and the retreat, the position of defense. For the last ten years, on average, you process eight to twenty times more information a day. Today, everybody gets fired several times in their life, "mobbing," burn-out, we all go through this, it's normal.

You have to know how to mourn the loss of a job, and how to be resilient if you don't want to sink. In the phases when you are in a hole, it can happen that you don't want to go out anymore, that you're frightened by people. You don't want to see your friends anymore because you reflect back to them the Sword of Damocles weighing over their heads, and they remind you that you've been ejected. Ali saw people collapse; it can lead all the way to death. More generally, you have to be open minded—if you're demanding, you vanish into oblivion—show your will to learn, be flexible. You have to be willing to access information. It's the same for everyone. You have to determine the habits that can block your life. When she's stressed at work, Denise goes to the bathroom to do breathing exercises. She also takes yoga classes and goes swimming to unwind, because otherwise she doesn't hold up.

The train is starting again. We've arrived at the station, the doors are opening, but you can't exit immediately because of these overcrowded tracks. If after two weeks the coaching does not bring any results, Samuel recommends entering the second phase: two months in a fake company. They exist in all shapes and sizes, between twenty and two thousand employees. You wake up every morning to go to work in the fake company, spending the day with your fake colleagues, processing files, answering the phone, solving problems, developing communication strategies to launch new products, on both a national and international scale. It's a highly developed network, you can contact your fake colleagues everywhere in the world to close fake deals. Stranded in this crowd on the track: the AC has just shut down, the electric system of the entire station has just shut down. The heat is so intense that my brain pauses, as if I could see myself from above. I stop thinking for just for a few seconds; it doesn't last long, tiny gaps, I hardly notice it. The heat is all over Europe I've heard. It has never been this hot before; 45 degrees in Rome says Brendan. It's even warmer in Athens; Adam is over there. Out of the subway station in the open air, my body regains its standard mode of functioning very fast, it takes only a few seconds; I walk up the street and here is John.

7.

Juliana would fake orgasm with her ex-boyfriend for the first time in her life: I join her for coffee, and she has just broken up with him. The only thing she wants is that he block her, on Instagram. She would post some little jokes about him, and he would totally flip out on her. He was always so nice in public, and abusive in private. That's the worst, because your friends are like, he's so nice! Those guys don't make good love to you, and then they scream at you. The sex was terrible; he would have all sorts of excuses for bad sex, ready to go. It was all about insecurity. He wanted to have the public image of a hot couple, and then he was jealous of the Instagram comments. After they broke up, even his best friend tried to hang out with her because he thought she was a star on Instagram. He called her a bitch. That's why she left. A self-centered bitch that spent her days Photoshopping herself.

Then he apologized fifteen thousand times but she was like: "bye." She can deal with cheating, but this, abuse, she just can't work through it. It's like this: you accept it, you accept it, until one day, you don't accept it anymore. This game of power: you can reverse it, you don't really know how but one day, just like that, you say no and you take over.

She wanted to have coffee with him, to discuss how they were going to navigate the breakup, and all she wanted was that he block her. Once he'll have blocked her, she would be good. She just wants him to block her, that's all she asks. She blocked him so he can't see her, but she still sees his shit, she wants him to block her, that's it.

He was so frustrated, and watching so much porn. His porn rate was insane. A lot of repression, raised Irish Catholic. Having sex once with a Muslim for example: he would take a shower right after, apologizing, saying that it usually didn't happen, please don't say it to anyone! Religion brainwashes you in such a strong way, makes you feel guilty about all your fantasies: the Madonna-whore rage. Just angry with yourself, with men, with women, and then you start treating everyone badly.

When Juliana was younger, people would make fun of her all the time. It's not that she didn't like her body, but she was kind of forced not to like her body because of how people responded to it. Her mom was more like, whatever it takes to make you look like a normal boy. So they wanted her to have surgery when she was 16, they were going to remove her breasts and get her testosterone injections because her estrogen level was too high. The doctors in her town, they didn't really know. They didn't even process the idea that she could be intersex. She figured it out by herself. They were about to put her on steroids, and go through surgery to remove all the breast tissue from her body. They also had some weird workout plans.

The only reason it didn't happen is because her dad refused to sign the papers. She's so happy she didn't have this crazy surgery. Because she didn't know at the time, when you're 16 you do what people tell you to. She was like: whatever it takes to make me just walk through life and not feel weird. So she researched online and found these chest binders to hide her breasts. She would wear a lot of layers, three, four, up to five layers.

Changing rooms were always awkward, because she was in the boy's locker room and all the boys kept looking at her and got turned on. She would just hide in a corner. Her mom would force her to do things with boys to make her normal: like typical boy's sports, or she would have to go to these sleepovers. At that age, boys are so stupid, they have weird hormones, and they'd do things, like when she was sleeping they would masturbate on her and she would wake up with the cum all over, they would grab her boobs, and jerk off on her. She was so angry. She had dried cum on her. They were like animals. She always thought she was a girl. College was better, very few people knew: "I'm gonna move to New York, and let my body be free."

And that's what happened. She moved to New York. At 21, she started the hormones, the estrogens. She already has estrogen but she also has testosterone. It makes her feel much better, she feels better in her body. She sometimes thinks about removing her penis but besides the fact that it's fourteen thousand dollars, she doesn't really need this surgery. They remove the testicles; technically it's not a removal of the penis, it's more like inverting it. Originally everyone has both. So they just reverse it. For a long time, people thought you have to go through surgery, but today, it's more like you can be a woman and have a penis.

The estrogen changes your mood, how you are, how you feel. You can get really emotional after a shot, but usually you're calmer, less anxious. Now she feels when it's happening and she just says to people: watch out, it's happening! She feels so much happier in her body. No more conflict. She thinks it changed how she orgasms. Ham to that! She has two kinds of orgasm, the one when she literally comes, and the one when it's about getting to the orgasmic state. This can develop all life long: you can even have it in dreams, without even touching yourself, it comes from the brain. Or when it happens over and over several times: you can have sex for so long. You can do so many different things and it only gets better. When you know what you like, you take responsibility for your fantasies, you feel much more confident, you just let it go.

You can be a dom: you don't let anyone touch your body. You're closed when you do that. Or you can be submissive as well, that's very personal. You learn how to tie the balls, the technical side, flogging practice—if you hit there, that's the kidney, so it might get dangerous. There are some tricks: how to bend someone from the neck to the balls, the butt, the hands. Sex can be crazy. It's a therapy. You work through so much personal shame, gender shame, racial shame, thanks to this practice.

Juliana had a partner; they worked through everything. She still thinks she's indebted to him a lot. The second he told her "I love you," it happened in one night, she became his girlfriend, then the Madonna, and it was over. Just after that one night when they had the craziest sex ever. They went through everything. She got violently dark. She could not believe she was doing that, they were confronting so many taboos, all night long. She asked him to call her a nigger. It was liberating.

You can also wear the craziest outfit, ousting sex, sweating sex; it changes how you behave. That experience makes you completely change how you relate to your body in terms of presentation. Doing it with two men: that's the best. To be totally penetrated, feeling two men inside of you. It's so intense. The masochism, to feel pain is actual therapy. Confronting your fears. It's life changing. You have your sessions; you work through everything. Punch you, kick you, chuck you, chain you, weird race things: chained like a slave, to be fucked like a whore. The pain aspect is separate from the role-playing. It's addictive because it's intense, powerful because you realize that what you fear isn't that bad, and you can move through it. The thing with pain is that it goes away. Pain doesn't last that long, it's so fast, once you realize that, you're the most powerful, you start to want more and more and more. It can go all the way to bleeding, but it's also a performance. The submissive is the one who leads. You can get high from that. When you're in that subconscious state, you're being asked what you want: I want to be called a slut. I want to be called a nigger. To be treated like a slave. Sex is rebellion. Sex is a source of freedom and when you've reached that point you usually don't need it that way anymore. As a woman you're trained to be ashamed of being bold with your sexual desire, so it's great to go through this experience, to have someone call you a disgusting slut. Because it allows you to voluntarily get over it. You can also use another language when you do that, it's liberating. As a woman or as a black person you're trained to be respectable: "I don't sleep with too many men, only when I'm in love. I'm a good person. I'm not a slut. I'm smart, hard-working. I went to Bard. I'm teaching at EPFL..." So it's about this, but it's also about challenging the other person to take on his role as a dom. For example with a white old man, so that he will over-identify with his subjectivity. There is a lot of guilt doing it to a woman and even more to a black body. Let's both be liberated by the place we are at in history. Because most people don't want to do that but the impulse is there, you carry it with you, so it forces you to punch that out:

"They're going crazy about closing the coffee shop. Let's take a selfie with the selfie stick and leave."

"I'm in love with that object. I'm obsessed with the selfie stick. Ok, more angles, try to move more that way, in front of this wall, perfect, closer together, good. Let's take the two-second countdown. Ok, let's do another one with that angle. Yes that's good. Let me see: ham! And another one a little bit closer. Yes to that! It's a really good photo! Then you can tan in a row, you can add a filter. This one is nice. The hands are good. It just gets the perfect angle with the stick. This is cute: let's post this one. I want the bluetooth selfie stick one with the remote on it. I need to upgrade to the bluetooth one. I feel so ridiculous when I pull it out: Oh, I love Instagram!"

8.

Pati's vodka business is operational, from production to distribution. The quality of the product, the shape of the bottle, the logo, the labels, the cost of production and the sales price—she hired a consultant specialized in the area of liquor to work on the numbers—so as to make them accessible and understandable to potential investors, who must understand quickly where their money goes. Investing your own money is not recommended, convincing investors is a crucial step: the product needs to be confronted to this reality in order to start to exist.

Pati is a lawyer, it happened a bit by accident, she was hesitating between law and architecture. In college she was already interested in the system of justice. Since you have to choose what you want to do right after school, and she had no idea, law or architecture seemed to be two options that remained more or less open and it left her the possibility of choosing later. People often hesitate between law and architecture also because they are both serious options, which provide security. And law is interesting because there are always many truths. The problem is that people lie. They lie about everything all the time.

Untangling lies and reality by collecting information, then managing to convince: the law provides basic tools for all kinds of activities. You don't even have to become a lawyer, although that's what she did, but since it wasn't really what she wanted to do, she developed other activities in parallel. She'd started to work as a curator at the end of her studies in West Germany, where she was born. She never really realized that the Berlin wall had fallen; she was twelve years old. Going to the forest on weekends, it was not something she missed, because she simply never thought about it. She was used to travelling long distances to leave the city, taking that route and crossing through the country without stopping, that's the way it was, she'd never known anything else.

She doesn't regret having left Berlin for New York, has kept her habits and hardly leaves the city, doesn't go on holiday; with her three jobs she doesn't have time and she can't stand to sit idly. She wakes up every day at 7:45 a.m. The trip is the same; the landscape changes. It has always changed but it changes faster and faster: within a few months, a kiosk can become a fast-food joint, a coffee shop, a clothing store, a beauty salon, a yoga studio, a bar, and a bakery.

You can find everything at Billy's, everything that is sugary; biscuits, cakes, cupcakes, of all kinds and sizes, in all possible frosting combinations, of all colors, and for every taste: pumpkin with cinnamon cream cheese, pumpkin with carrot, carrot with cream cheese or without, classic chocolate with chocolate, yellow daisy with chocolate, apple crumb, hazelnut, white chocolate and cranberry, gluten free dark chocolate with banana cream, banana Nutella, peppermint icebox cake, blue-white-red cupcake (to Pray for Paris), peanut-butter jelly, plain, butter chocolate, Red Velvet cupcake with cream cheese frosting (for Breast Cancer Awareness Month), blue, green, yellow, orange or brown frosting, pumpkin bar, Snickerdoodle, gluten free chocolate chip, butterscotch gingerbread, lemon cranberry, oatmeal raisin, and much more. The coffee shop display at the front of the shop is a bit strange. Observing this weird front window from the inside, you don't really believe in it, the tables and the chairs are only there for decoration, nobody ever sits in them. You realize pretty fast that the back of the store, used for cake production, is much bigger than the front, which welcomes the clients. Queuing at the counter inside the giant front window and picking your cupcake, you can hear dozens of voices, people working in the back, making the cakes and the frosting. Most of the products are sold online. All day long, delivery people come and go past this giant front window, on bicycles, by car, or on foot, to pick up the cakes and distribute them all over the city. The cakes are carefully wrapped: a very particular attention is given to the presentation.

Léonard sees everything in terms of packaging: these Italian biscuits that are placed on this table, for example, have been wrapped by hand in silk paper. A medicine box: the name of the medicine is printed in letters, but the label is also inscribed in Braille. So when you film it, you don't see anything. That is, if there is a mistake on the packaging, you don't see it, and you run the risk of being sued.

The most complicated to handle is the Braille. One mistake and you can kill someone. Then, a suit will follow. How can you make sure that what the label says is correct? Léonard is working on developing a control system with dozens of lasers: the rays are deviated by the small bubbles of Braille, the information is transmitted to detectors that analyze it and tell you if the bubbles are in the right place. The cardboards come out at a speed of six hundred meters a second, minimum. In one second, ten meters come out, so you don't see anything.

Léonard works in the department that produces the sensors: he is developing sensors that can light up with LEDs at regular intervals. An image is taken every 25 micro-seconds. Today, every-thing is filmed so it's a hundred percent guaranteed. Every cardboard stock that comes out is guaranteed one hundred percent, so you can be sure it's good. The paper is filmed before it is folded, at six hundred meters a minute, and you can guarantee 100% that they are all good: ok—ok—ok—ok—ok. When one isn't good—for example if the letter S is missing—it is chucked away, the chain is interrupted, and starts up immediately. Before, one piece of card-board stock out of twenty used to be checked; it was picked up randomly and checked. Today, you can check them all.

Those machines are meant to create a product that is torn, on average, within twelve to thirteen seconds after purchase. Four bil-lion annual sales. This company holds 56% of packaging market shares worldwide: medicine labels, wavy cardboard stock, or the kind of bag used for potato chips. Half of the world's packaging is created by their machines. They don't produce the stock, only the machines. Developing a product is good, but then you have to be able to industrialize it, and to have it circulate throughout the world: for example, if you can't produce at least 2.5 million a week, there's no point to having invented it. The company sets itself apart from the competition because it's the only one capable of building machines which offer a hundred percent guarantee.

The card stock comes out as sheets, which will be folded into a box, which will go into a bigger box of six, then in a bigger box of twenty-four, then on a pallet, then in a truck. If the prepared folds of the card stock are not at the right place when you fold it, it will be a bit too big in one direction so in the box of six it becomes a bit annoying, and so on, until you can't manage to fit them in the truck, and then you lose money. Léonard develops machines that guarantee that all the prepared folds are well made.

If a sheet is not well made it gets ejected. He is developing a sensor that continuously takes pictures and that can tell if the fold has been made in the right place. The measuring time between pictures is twenty-five thousandths of a microsecond. About one second divided by a million. So you shoot photos at the rate of twenty-five millionths of a second. The lighting is so violent that when you test the prototypes, you have to wear a welder's mask: it's like a fire bowl.

Locked in his studio, Seth is testing a new machine, a camera mounted on an articulated arm with a large chain fixed on every side of the table by two feet. It moves slowly above a body lying on a massage table and held down by a belt, today it surveys a shaved man's leg. Cables tell the machine to move this way, or go up and down, the system makes sure everything is in focus. Everything here, here and there is in focus. The camera is fixed to a robot that is fixed to the feet, a dozen cables link the machine to a processor that is linked to a computer, the articulated arm unwinds slowly, a few millimeters every second, slowly zigzagging along the skin—he's using it for skin, to take pictures of skin. It's a bit transparent.

The camera flashes about once every second, thousands of times a day, it sounds like a clock. There are about one and a half terabytes of raw material produced each day. The camera takes thousands of pictures of every part of the body, following a preprogrammed drawing and rhythm. For example, for the drawing of the arm, the arm is divided into squares; it's a kind of grid that the machine follows. It's like a strange robot. It's a camera controlled by software, so it moves very methodically, you can tell it exactly where to take pictures; any specific part of your body can be in focus.

We walk by the window and discuss the bar, both of us looking outside: he asks me where the name comes from—you can't pronounce it—something like Vjjjjjzzzhh. He says my name: JjeAnNe!

I wonder how to pronounce his: Sett, SeFth, SesS, and ask him where he grew up. He takes his pencil off his ear and draws a line on the window frame with three points: he was born stateless, grew up in Boston, studied in Rhode Island, has lived in New York for twenty years. It's a five hour drive along the East Coast: this is the coast, the water is here, and this is the land. "Jjeann, if you could choose a size for this compass, what would it be?" He points to a pile of stones outside that are being charged onto a truck, a few dozen meters below us: we wonder where the stones are going. Probably from one pile in Manhattan to another pile in Brooklyn, Queens, or the Bronx, piles endlessly moved around. They are building something new over there in that hole: soon we won't see the *Empire State Building* anymore. We won't see anything anymore.

9.

We go out to the Fee Glacier's subway station with Sylvère. At 3,500 meters altitude, this is the highest subway in the world, but in reality it's more of a funicular: two kilometers of tunnel bored into mountain and ice, with an elevation change of five hundred meters. The subway leads to the highest revolving restaurant in the world, 2,000 meters above the village, the path is so steep that we nearly get stuck at the top, Sylvère has made a picnic, the undercooked eggs get crushed and explode all over the sandwiches.

These streets are steep, they rise and fall sharply. Early in the morning, the Koreans come to exercise in the park, and then later the Mexicans. The neighborhood is mixed. The residents are half and half, white and Latino, but that's changing. Originally, at the turn of the century, this was a really nice neighborhood, while East LA was pretty dangerous—*this* was West LA, meaning west relative to the area farther east. Silver Lake: there are all these small restaurants now, that's recent. Macarthur Park: before, we never even went there, didn't even step foot! And this street with small businesses of all kinds, on the weekends people sell whatever, the sidewalk flooded with all kinds of everyday items: Sylvère walks around here every day, everybody does, everybody who doesn't have a car. The contractors came to build city apartments here, so that people could live near where they worked. Koreatown, everyone has cars there, it's six or seven blocks away, and here is an ancient Jewish deli, serving typical kosher dishes, and these here are traditional Mexican blankets, they are made in Hong Kong.

It's very unstable right now, it's uncertain. It's not a panic, but it's full of invisibility. Here you cut from Alvarado to Sunset, the main road connecting Echo Park and Silver Lake. Here is the *one oh one*, the Hollywood highway that runs north-south. Here everyone has a car: if there isn't another crisis, it will become like Silver Lake, it already has. Sunset spans the entire city from east to west. There is the *one oh one* that goes toward the north—not *to* the north but *toward* north—and then there is the *one ten*, that goes to the north, to Pasadena, plus the 5 Freeway, which runs north-south. Between all these, you always find a route. Here there were hundreds of balloons of many colors and sizes floating all around, this lake is split in half by the road. You feel right away when there is water.

It's the same with the hail, Noé feels hail right away, you can stop it with rockets: 1,500 meters high, loaded with a kilo of explosives. Inside there are two materials; on one side explosives, on the other a silver that stops the formation of the hailstones, dissolves the pellets, makes them melt. They did that for twenty years in the middle of the night, launched rockets into the clouds. They didn't really know if it was useful so they stopped, and they still don't know what effect it had on the weather, the wind currents are so violent when the hail storms come in from the Rhône Valley, the rockets were dangerous because sometimes they wouldn't start: you would light the fuse and it wouldn't launch. The instructions were to take it, gently, and submerge it in a sink, in water, so it wouldn't explode. You do that twice, but then you don't want to leave an arm, a leg, or half a head on a rocket. The rockets had a launch range up to 2,000 meters.

The funicular to Victoria Peak: 900 meters elevation change. It's really steep. Suspended on a cable, you have to be seated or else you'll spill around inside the tramcar. All the seats are positioned the same direction, facing the slope, so that when you are seated your neck hurts and the blood rises to your head. You arrive at a station located directly inside the shopping mall dug into the peak, you climb six escalators to reach the top: no one can see there. Even Juliana's flash catches all the fog. I never thought fog could be so intense that you can't see at all.

Does anyone want to see the fog from here? Let's go down to the first floor. The walking path might be on the first floor. No, we want to go this way, that is a trap, we can't get out there. It smells like crack here, someone just smoked crack on that hill. It smells like shit in the lobby. They're probably running out of perfume. Everyday they spray it all over the lobby. It smells so good, there have been three different scents since we've arrived! You can like breathe guilt free! Everything looks clear, I feel that my vision is clear now, the air is clearer: I can, like, see buildings!

I don't understand, it's just such a weird object as a building, there are doors on the facade: Stewart has always been curious about what happens inside. He went there once, with his assistant, and when you go inside, there is a door, and then there is another door that is completely closed, it looks like a microwave, it has the same dimensions as a microwave, many spaces have these proportions, or you feel like you're in a fridge. Refrigerators are like this, vertical, and microwaves are horizontal, microwaves are never tall. So you walk into this very small space and there is just a door in front of you and you can't open it, and then to your right it's all tiled, like a bathroom, but there is a small area with three little holes. And somebody is like, hello! from these three little holes, and you're like, what? You can't even see inside, because they are looking at you through a camera, a voice says the rate, by the hour, for two or for twenty-four hours.

Heike's new house is at the end of this garden, there are two front doors next to each other, so you can choose one. They've been here for dozens of years, from the time it was still a nursery, she has poured a concrete floor and put in windows that were stored in her cellar into the wooden walls; the window in the brick wall was already there, it looks into the shower of the exercise room inside, you can still see men showering through the window. So, two front doors, in the first room there is a small table with a built-in bench that must have been used by the nursery's children, another door with a sticker from a phone box, and a giant chimney along one wall made from brick, it's thirty meters high, it will still be there in a hundred years.

Those belong to the new owners: this is going to be a really cute Thai restaurant in a few weeks. I really like the toilet door though, I want to keep the toilet door. Matthew has tons of furniture in his house that he has to fix. An entire room filled with furniture. He has been doing it on and off for a long time, a few years ago he got into it, fixing and selling furniture. Now he's more picky, he buys Swedish teak from the '70s and '80s because it's kind of ugly, so people don't like it and get rid of it. It's an unstable business, and can be really distracting because you have to look at everything.

Kiki's scar goes through her chest, from her lower abdomen to sternum, she has an unusual tolerance for pain, that's why her appendix swelled up so much inside her belly, she almost died, she needed surgery to be opened and have the pieces removed one by one, she wears thick glasses, lives in downtown Beijing: it's all finance buildings here. It's good to live here because it's the city center. She doesn't wear a mask, but sleeps with an air purifier. She likes the smog, that's why Beijing is so addictive: you die a little bit, but you want more. The most important thing is to have clean air while you're sleeping, the rest of the day you don't really care. The windows are cleaned weekly but because of the smog they're always black so you don't really see through them, it doesn't matter so much because it's the same outside, you can hardly see. It rains every day at noon for thirty minutes, with the rockets you can do that, they are launched into the sky to make the water fall and clean the air. Black rain falls every day at the same time on the windows, that's why they are so dirty.

10.

I'll take the new car out and you park the old one instead, ok? It's silent, 100% electric. We have to be careful, we are silent. The pedestrians, the cyclists: we move but nobody can hear us. The car doesn't smell like anything, as if it was dead. We still have 83 kilometers of autonomy. You never have to tank. The car does it on its own. Everybody is as fast and as silent as we are now. This street is blocked. They found a 100 kilo bomb from World War II, that often happens in Berlin. On Schönleinstrasse, there was nothing, we were living here, look, our flat is still in that building on the 3rd floor, the street seems to be longer now, we also lived here, on Linienstrasse; the city is a construction site but it has calmed down these last few years. All of Unter den Linden Avenue is an open trench right now, you can see the pipes inside.

I see this book at the supermarket, *Nie wieder chaos, das Haushalt im Griff haben.* "Cool," I think, and put it in my pocket. I like this club, half of the crowd is perverse. Frank has been a doorkeeper for twenty years, he recognizes everyone. He was already at the door at the Pogo. Ken and Nick were there too, so did Pati. We must have seen each other but we didn't know each other then. I knew Heike, but I didn't know them yet. John and I were both at

Genesis's concert for the New Year in 2000, but we didn't know each other yet.

That guy in red who just passed by, jogging along the lake right in front of us, I know him, he's from Montréal. I heard he was living here but we aren't in contact anymore. I'm sure it was him. I've known him since nursery school. My ears recognized him. I heard someone say "jeudi soir," and immediately recognized the accent, "jeudi souar," "jeudi soère." There is a kind of moment of latency. It's bizarre. You've just arrived a few hours ago in a city and the first person you run into is someone you know. You don't want to say hi. Reconnecting with someone from school after ten or twenty years puts you in a weird state. You both left the same place. Then you see the person again. You've changed. And when you look at each other, you see yourself as you were ten years before. As if two different people who've always known each other were meeting for the first time.

I was here twenty years ago, on this island. It's the first time I've come back and I don't remember anything except the swimsuit that I was wearing, white with red starfish. I saw you from far away. I wasn't sure it was you because you were wearing a new bath suit. This woman, she looks like a friend, but from ten years ago. She's dressed exactly the same way as ten years ago. The waitress is wearing the same shorts as you, look, they are exactly the same. Our new neighbor is going to open a restaurant in Berlin. Like Marie. Are you sure it's not Marie? I think she would have recognized us. I recognize him, he used to do autopsies. As for her, it feels like she has been stitched back up.

I couldn't see for twenty years. Or only things I chose. Because I was only able to see a little, I could only see the things I'd chosen. Eight cornea transplants. You see with someone else's cornea. Then the body rejects it, the one after the other. One day, you don't know why, the body doesn't want it anymore and you have to start all over again. Today, the left side is stable but they've done so many surgeries on the right eye that the cornea fell out. The eye couldn't take it anymore. The problem was pressure on the eye. The surgeon invented a tool that could reach behind the cornea: suddenly you can see everything and you're shocked. Then it starts over again. You miss a step, two weeks later, you hit a door and you hardly see anything anymore. When you don't see, your senses change. You recognize people by smell, the sound of feet in the stairs. The New York subway still has the same smell, after all these years, it's exactly the same smell.

11.

This bridge is very old. This is the Harlem Bridge, it was built in the '30s to bring water into the city and they cleaned it last year. This park is very old. Completely derelict, it's wild now. Look down, dozens of meters below, these stairs that zigzag, they lead to the highway and down to the river littered with empty bottles, plastic bags. This trash seems to have been there forever. This old streetlamp without a head, you can see inside it: dead leaves, rotten wires, and rusted metal. The berries in that bush are bleached, but they are not supposed to be bleached! I've never seen that color before! This high wall above us has fallen down, it was built with bricks, something else must have been there a long time ago. It makes you think of this movie. Have you seen it? There is a corpse in a park. They could have shot it here a long time ago. I think they shot this other movie here, their family house must not be so far, it could be this one, a few blocks away. These houses used to be very far from the city.

Further down from that bridge, you see Columbia over there. Below, see this huge hole? It's ready to welcome new construction. They are planning to build a whole new building. It will be huge. There used to be a good restaurant down there, in that other hole and these green gates, they lead to a waste facility. The marble statue in this nail salon, he's too big, he fills this entire room. They do everything here, manicures, eyelash extensions, waxing, facial masks, massages. This bar is completely empty, there are maybe twenty people in this huge hall, these cafés are new, this is the Symphony: I saw a concert there in the '80s. Do you know this song? It's a beautiful song, Fitzgerald used to live here in that building, he was an alcoholic, he wrote *The Crack-Up* in there: see, these little houses used to be very far from the city, too.

If you could live in one of these two buildings, which one would it be? This one has probably been built for offices; this is a real deco building, it's beautiful, it's huge. This bar is very old, it's the oldest bar in the city. They used to make the signs like that, hand painted, you see? These fruits and vegetables displayed everywhere: this was the largest fruit stand in the city for a very long time, it's famous, you recognize it immediately. This is a typical Jewish place, you can see this guy ordering, it's typical. Broadway is the longest street in the city, it runs all across the city, its path was already used by the Indians even before the colonizers arrived, it goes all the way downtown, that's why it has this shape that's not straight, that's why they built the Flatiron Building: this building, I love this building, it's elegant. This was built in the '60s, this is the old library, right here you have the Shake Shack, it's a place for burgers, this is an old dive bar, it has been here since forever. This is new, the health care center, you just go there, it's like a shop for the first treatment, so you don't have to wait or anything, if something happens to you, you just go in there: City Care.

Did you ever have an eating disorder? Kentucky Fried Chicken, they might not be able to use that name anymore since you're not sure if these animals are still chickens. It's fake chicken, at least, or something else. This gym was the first one built in the city, it's a private club, that's an old, very old, building, you can try to get in it, just to get a view, to take a look at what it's like. It doesn't look like a gym at all. They have things like restaurants and dining rooms inside, it's a big club. You have to be invited by a member to get in. You have to find out who the members are. This is a beautiful hotel, its bar is beautiful, you feel good in here. The walking-dead barkeeper has been working here for a century. He's old, you can hear it, his voice trembles:

"You will both sit at the Philip Johnson table, he used to sit there in that corner, this was his table. He's dead now."

So we're on Lexington now. Let's rest here for a while. This is the DoubleTree hotel. The Korean street, the hairdresser's street, it has been there since the '60s, it's very crowded, these buildings, you imagine there are a lot of hospital workers living here—like you're from Pakistan, and you get your first job in the city and end up here. These are typical modern buildings, look how the three of them are spaced, they haven't been touched since then, all the apartments still have the same curtains, their square windows look like television sets. The suicide library, it appeals to suicides, this huge staircase, if you would have been studying here, you would have certainly committed suicide. See, it's a real vampire, you can see him through the window, sitting in this fast food place with his gray skin, this bar is very old, it opened in the '80s, its New York-French style is from the '80s, they used to paint walls eggshell white then, to make places look more French. Put your legs over me and rest: if you could choose a color for the wall of your bar, which one would it be?

You've mistaken this clothing store for a bar! It's not a bar at all! Here, this is Max Fish, it moved recently, it's a legendary old place, the light is bright, it feels like a hole, they moved the decorations, it's like being back in the '90s with this music and all these kids. Do you know this fish? It's a strange creature, the sunfish, very old, from another age. Look at this, it's giant, it's a hundred gallons, it's called "Rubbermaid," that's written on it. You can put all kinds of stuff in there. I'll bring you one so you can put your books inside. That store with these bright lights must be a hundred meters high, in China you have a few fake Apple stores too, hundreds of people work there, wearing fake t-shirts and selling fake iPhones, nobody knows who they're actually working for, they all think they're working for Apple, but they're probably working for you.

This white building, it was built for you, your name is written on it. Imagine all these people living in there, all these windows; this building, it's for all your children. This new sidewalk with these large gray asphalt squares you are walking on, it was made just for you. Your hair is floating all over the city.

12.

This is the old town, this used to be the city here, it was the center, there were farms up there. Don't walk in the dead leaves, there are rats in these leaves for sure, they cleaned the park, it used to be like in the movie *Kids*: that's this park. This arch is a memorial for George Washington, the first president of the United States. It's at the bottom of Fifth Avenue. That's 1 Fifth Avenue. It's very, very expensive now. It's the most expensive neighborhood. Have you seen the movie *Ghostbusters*? The ghosts were in there. That used to be a really good video rental store, that was the first Japanese restaurant, I used to go there in the '80s, it's still there. This is a foam store, they make custom foam. It's still there. I have a couch made from this foam. What happened to this park? They redesigned it! Wait! I've been here before! This used to be something else!

It's nice in the park right here because there are different levels to walk, and here you have the hippos, here are the crabs under the obelisks, and look at this dog, his eye has sunk into his head, that must be a hybrid dog, it looks like a sheep, no way his body is big enough to support that head, this is Broadway again, it goes all the way down, you walk all the way down and you cross the entire city. I've gone to that park before, I've been here before but it was something else!

This is weird, it's going to be cold again, you can't trust this, it's too warm, this is a building from the 2000s, this used to be something else, this used to be on Penn but it moved!

Here is the oldest place for bagels, the light is a bit green, it hasn't changed in forever, it's built a bit higher, on rocks, not on garbage, so it can't be flooded. This building was beautiful, wavy, it just burnt down, the fire started in the floor, between the planks. It has completely disappeared. It's really calm here, you hear nothing. And the air is better. You breathe better. I really thought these children were horses in my side vision. Families, that's the most important force in this neighborhood: babies.

Can you ride a bicycle? Because you can ride all the way down the highway. It's not far. It used to be very far, but it's not anymore. I've heard my favorite restaurant is moving just next door. The elevator is so slow, as if every floor were thirty meters tall. Sometimes the express train acts funny at night, something is different, the city has flipped, it's turned upside down, everything used to be very far, not like now, and here the Symphony, it's becoming a gym.

I thought there was a Citibank over there. There was, but it has closed! It looks like there is one, let me see, wait there is one, there is one further up, if you walk this way. It's close, it's so close—we're almost there—oh it's so close. I love the shape of that building over there, it's great. I hate this train station, it's so crowded, it's super crowded, okay here we are, street level, it's supposed to be over here, right here, okay we're almost there. I love our comfortable shoes, listen, there is no sound when we walk, they are totally silent, I love walking silently.

From here you can usually see the bridge, but we can't see anything today, the weather is too bad. To go to the printer, it's not far, you take the subway, you change seven times from the Hutong, seven different airs: the red alarm started yesterday, it's so bad that you can't breathe outside. It's more than a thousand, but you don't know of what exactly, here everyone has this app where you can check the weather and air conditions. When they say the weather is nice it doesn't mean it's sunny, it means you can see. Whether you can see or not, breathe or not: that's because of the air pollution. The air can be foggy, like a haze, a white dense thing, like cotton, when it has a taste and a smell; that's the smog.

Then you can't see anything, it burns when you breathe. Winter is the worst because of the coal, March is better. Spring is usually very windy. Because it's also related to the geography, this wind only comes once every week or two with the mountains and the desert around. There are a lot of rumors, it's very complicated to know. You can have these air cleaning machines in your room to protect yourself when you sleep, everyone has one. Or you can live in these networks of homes with purified air so you don't have to breathe outside. Usually I just don't go out when it's like that. Today is nice because of the wind, it's good quality air, but yesterday was terrible, you couldn't see. You feel it, you're in a bad mood, it burns a bit, you're coughing, it tastes funny.

If you go that way, that's the city. This bar has been here for two years, I thought it wouldn't last for a month, it's always empty, it doesn't look like anywhere, they shoot a lot of movies in here, you're never sure if it's reality or a movie when you enter. This is a good place to eat, and here is this other hotel, that's all new, these huge buildings, they built them two years ago, look we see the sun! You see over there? This bar, it's just an exact copy of that other bar, so it feels like you're there but it's just another one, a one-to-one copy. They copied everything, but this one is actually more crowded, I think I prefer this one. As long as you stay in the village you don't need that many things. Here you can buy fruits, and here it's nice to eat in that small restaurant. They're building the new subway very fast, soon it will be here but it hasn't come yet. So you don't go to the city that much, you don't want to do that if you don't really have to. This area would be really nice if it had some green—maybe the Great Wall will have some green. You see the mountains? They're much greener. I have this headache again, the air is bad, but the gray is nice, I prefer gray because when it's too white it's depressing.

Are we near a rubber factory? It smells like rubber, I'm not sure. I love the casual wearing of face masks. I'm a bit lazy with masks, I start only at two hundred, it's just annoying to talk. Anyway it's hard to know when to wear one. With the coughing you can know how the air is, or I look at the color and feel the texture, or smell how it tastes. I like the gray, it depends, when it's white-gray, pale, *blême*, bleached.

When the sandstorms hit, then you really want to wear the mask. I've heard that the desert is coming. In six years, it will be here, then the city will have to move. They are building a new city, the mega city, it already exists, connecting three cities together; they are building high-speed trains, so it will make everything smaller. A hundred and thirty million people will live there.

Is that a real dog? This area is like a jail, it looks like a prison, I wonder what was here before, I think it was a garden two hundred years ago. This is probably an old building, it looks so old. I can't believe the sky is blue today, I wonder what happened. Clean the air! Clean the air! Clean the air for the committee! Is that the Forbidden City? It looks like its back door, it's hard to tell where to enter. Some parts seem so old, like they're not real anymore. That's so funny, these buildings, fifteen years ago, they looked like the newest thing; now they're so decrepit, they look so old. Everything that's taller was built after the '90s. I love this place—it's half nail salon, half flower shop—it smells so good, and I love to put my fingers in this weird light thing.

This food makes me sleepy, it happens really fast. I can't deal with you just making noise and fake talking, we need to find someone we can show the phrase on the phone to so we can find that place. I'll remember the building when we're in front of it: maybe it's over here, oh yeah it's over here, this is it. These small roads are tucked away, isn't that where we just went? It looks exactly the same. Isn't that the same sign? I remember this building. I think this is a trap, I don't think we'll get out there. It feels so hazy, it's bizarre, I don't know what's going on, it's so empty, silent, the air is like a pill, I feel sleepy, I feel like I'm sleepwalking right now, I was supposed to meet Yuan but she felt asleep, I would love to live in that house, it's cute.

Unconsciously you check, yes unconsciously you think about it all the time, you check, you arrive at the station and you check everything. You look. Montparnasse, it's the only tower in the city, and everybody hates it, the entire city hates this tower, there is a heliport on the roof, and a train station in the basement, it's between two boulevards, the *boulevard de l'arrivée* and the *boulevard du départ*. I will settle down there to do watercolors. Everyday you arrive, you put down your gun, you don't enter the tower without passing through the security check. You're there, you do your watercolors, you're chilling, you have twenty square meters, it's like being in a sauna all day long, or even in an aquarium, or like when it rains all day. Always in water. To use the brushes, to clean them, to dry them, you're telling yourself: I'm doing water painting, fine, but actually you are in water all the time. The water meter should indicate a lot more water. No need for a humidifier, you live in a heat chamber, a real sauna. To clean the boards, to stretch the papers, you're bathing in water all day long.

Do you want some cold water? Because it's really very hot. You put a ventilator in front of the window to make the cold air come in but it's still not enough, so then you drape a kind of curtain: you drench it completely so it's soaked with water, and three hours later it's dry. It's like glued to the thing and it leaves a mark, and you can't touch it either because it's too hot, it's like touching a hot plate, it hurts. Then you have to sleep with a sheet, like in the summer, it's 68°F, but it's more maybe, it must be around 30°C, the thermostat is regulated for an average temperature of twenty degrees, but because it's installed in a part of the building where it's cold, probably in the cellar, it's thirty degrees in the whole building.

John has just bought a carafe with a built-in filter, it's spilling all over the table and on the floor. He was fed up with all these plastic bottles that were laying around. The filter, you don't really know what's inside. The container got cracked, so it spills when you fill glasses, it's spilling on the table and it's making a huge puddle on the floor. It's really warm, and it's also humid because of these building's radiators, the one here's like a vampire that transpires, he's making steam, there is also a very little one in the bathroom it's like a sweet little animal, and this one it's like a beast, and the beast, she breathes. She breathes loud. They are puffing steam, all over the room, it's filling the entire apartment, and fogging up the windows.

I like it just after the rain. Always, like, right after. I really need to pull it together. I look puffier in the winter, people look puffier in the winter in general: puffy and flooded. In the sun your skin looks so good, everything is just cute, and you're sweating, so you're not overwatered all the time.

To John Kelsey, Anne Dressen, Juliana Huxtable, Sylvère Lotringer, Stefan Tcherepnin, AnnE Imhof, John Armleder, Mai-Thu Perret, Genesis Breyer P-Orridge, Amy Yao, Nicolas Ceccaldi, Seth Price, Olivia Creed, Fabrice Gygi, Catherine Chevalier, Patrick Galdemar, Anina Trösch, Romain Villet, Ibrahim Konaté, Nicolas Trembley, Brendan Mullane, Fabrice Stroun, Emanuel Rossetti, Linyao Kiki Liu, Matthew Langan Peck, Heike Dertmann, Frank Künster, Massimiliano Locatelli, Marie Karlberg, Stewart Uoo, Sam Pulitzer, Peter Wächtler, Daniel Dewar, Loren Muzzey, Pati Hertling, Nora Schultz, Léonard Badet, Ken Okiishi, Nick Mauss, Sophie Morner, Lionel Bovier, Isabelle Cornaro, Ericka Beckman, Noura Wedell, Hedi El Kholti, Chris Kraus, Adam Szymczyk, Cédric Bachelard, Carène Narbel, Paola Landolt, Marika Buffat, Paul-Aymar Mourgue d'Algue, Martin Schubart, Bruno Danese, Jaqueline Vodoz, Marie-France and Philippe Chopard Nordmann, Anaïs Verrey, Léonore, Alexandre, Christine, Michel, Aline, Pauline, Séverine, Emilie, Noémie, Noé, François and Malou Graff.

ABOUT THE AUTHOR

Writer and curator Jeanne Graff was born in Lausanne, Switzerland and lives in New York. She works in a vineyard, is columnist for *May Revue* (Paris), and teaches art school in Geneva at HEAD. In 2014, Graff founded 186f Kepler, an art space without walls. She has organized numerous international exhibitions, and performs with her band Solar Lice. Graff recently completed a writing residency at Villa Noailles in Hyeres, France.

VZSZHHZZ

Published by Semiotext(e)
PO BOX 629, South Pasadena, CA 91031
www.semiotexte.com

Cover Art: Hedi El Kholti, Mai-Thu Perret, Juliana Huxtable, Anina Trösch, John Kelsey, Jeanne Graff, Noé Graff.

Design: Hedi El Kholti

ISBN: 978-1-63590-015-6

Distributed by the MIT Press, Cambridge, MA, and London, England